ONE NIGHT BEFORE CHRISTMAS

by

SERENITY WOODS

ISBN: 9798302208088

CONTENTS

Chapter One

Astrid

I stand outside Midnight in Mayfair, the exclusive London members' club, and hunch my shoulders as Jack Frost tries to slide his icy fingers inside the collar of my jacket.

Music blasts out from inside, the thumping, sensual beat resonating in my bones. Two burly bouncers stand either side of the doors, denying entrance to the long queue of hopeful customers. The women are in stunning sequined gowns, while the guys—including the bouncers—are all wearing tuxedos.

I'm in jeans and a Christmas sweater my mum knitted for me with a picture of Rudolph and a sewn-on red pompom for his nose.

I tug my black jacket tighter around me and approach the bouncer on the left, who looks slightly less intimidating.

"Excuse me." My voice comes out as a squeak. He raises an eyebrow at me, so I clear my throat and try again. "Excuse me. I'm supposed to be working in the kitchen tonight. Can you tell me where I should go?"

Next to me, a woman in a tight black dress giggles, and I watch her whisper in her partner's ear. He grins, his gaze sliding down me, then returning to my blushing cheeks with amusement. The woman is stick thin. I can't believe she's ever eaten anything more than a lettuce leaf in her life. How does she fit all her organs into that skinny body?

I look back at the bouncer in time to see pity flicker on his features. "Around the back," he says, gesturing with his head down the alley next to the club. "The red door."

"Thank you." Lowering my gaze to the pavement, I turn the corner and stride along the alleyway.

It's so cold. A few flakes of snow flutter down, and my breath mists in front of my face. Immi has never made a snowman, so it's exciting that there's supposed to be a white Christmas this year.

I approach the red door. A bouncer stands here too, so presumably some guests must try to sneak in the back entrance. This guy smiles at me as I approach.

"Must be cold work standing around all evening," I say.

"I don't mind," he replies. "They pay well. Best security job I've had for years."

I return his smile. "I'm working in the kitchen tonight?"

"Sure thing. Go ahead." Clearly, I don't look like a customer trying to sneak her way in.

I open the door, go inside, and find myself in a large square foyer with several doors leading off either side. The place is bustling with people. To the left are a couple of swing doors with round windows, and as I watch, a waiter emerges carrying several plates of beautifully arranged food and heads along a corridor into what must be a restaurant. Two women, dressed in skimpy sequined outfits and high heels, come out of a door to the right and head up a wide, curving staircase, disappearing around the corner. People are constantly exiting one door and crossing to another, and everyone looks busy. A Christmas tree stands in one corner, decorated in red and gold, its fairy lights barely noticeable beneath the fluorescent strip lighting.

Ahead of me is what looks like an office. A tall woman is standing in the doorway talking to someone who's out of sight. Her black hair is cut in an extremely sharp bob, and she's wearing a black trouser suit with a white shirt. Something about her manner and the fact that she's carrying a clipboard suggests she's in charge.

Gathering my courage in both hands, I cross the foyer and approach her. She glances at me, and her eyebrows rise.

"Hello," I say. "I'm Astrid Bergman, from the Templeman Agency? They sent me to work in the kitchen tonight."

"Oh," she says, "yes, of course. I'm Miranda—I'm the Staff Manager here. Thank you for coming at such short notice. There's some kind of bug going around, and we've had several members of staff go down sick at the last minute."

"No problem at all," I say brightly. "Where should I go?"

Someone bumps into me, and I apologize and step closer to the office to get out of their way. As I do, I catch a glimpse of the person Miranda was talking to. He's huge—at least six four, I'd say, and with a build to match. He's dressed in a tux, but oddly he's also wearing a large black hoodie over the top. As he realizes I've seen him, he lifts the hood up over his head, but not before I catch sight of his face. About a third of it is covered with a stiff mask the same color as his light-brown skin. For a moment I wonder whether he's auditioning for Phantom of the Opera, but then he backs away into the shadows, suggesting that the mask covers a real injury, and guilt sweeps over me.

"I'll take you to the kitchen and introduce you to Chef Bernard," Miranda says, pronouncing it the French way. Of course, a member's club in Mayfair would have a French chef. I can't imagine how much membership costs.

Averting my gaze from the masked guy, I follow her across the foyer.

I'm just passing the sweeping staircase when a cry makes my head snap around. A young woman is descending the stairs in a hurry, and she must have missed a step, or maybe she put her foot down at the wrong angle, because she stumbles and pitches forward down the stairs.

I run forward and catch her at the bottom, just before she lands. The momentum of her fall pushes me back onto my butt, and we land in an untidy heap.

"Katie!" Miranda rushes up and helps the two of us disentangle our limbs. "Are you okay?"

Katie sits on the bottom step and presses her fingers to her mouth. She's gone as white as the snowflakes I can see through the windows, and she's trembling. "I rolled my ankle," she says. "Oh fuck. It really hurts!"

Trying not to think about how ungainly I must look, I get to my knees and move up to examine her ankle. "Ooh, that's going to be sore," I tell her as I see it already swelling. "You need to do the RICE thing—rest, ice, compression, and elevation. Then you'll be right as rain." I give her a reassuring smile.

"I'm supposed to be back on stage at seven," she says, her eyes shining as she looks at Miranda.

"I don't think that's going to happen," Miranda says briskly. "I'll get Carl to run you home, and…" She glances at me.

"Astrid," I remind her.

"Astrid here is right; you need to ice it and elevate it."

"I'm so sorry," Katie whispers. "I know you're short staffed at the moment."

"Don't worry about it. You concentrate on getting better." Miranda looks at me. "Can you get Carl? The bouncer outside?"

I run to the door, open it, and ask him to come in. Miranda instructs him to take Katie home, and he helps her up, then holds her as she limps to get her things.

Miranda watches them go, then looks at me and blows out a breath. "Just what we need," she murmurs.

"I'm not surprised she fell," I reply. "I'd break my neck in heels that high. And how does she dance in them? When I went to pole dancing classes, I had to do it barefoot."

Miranda chuckles, taking her phone out of her trouser pocket as it buzzes. She studies the screen, glances at her office, frowns, then answers it.

"Yes, sir? Did you go back upstairs? Oh, I'm sorry, Katie fell down the stairs, and I... oh, right. Yes, she's okay. I've asked Carl to take her home. I know, I was just saying that. I don't know. Eliza's sick, and Ruth can't come in tonight." Gradually, her gaze slides to me. "Astrid? No, sir, she came here to work in the kitchen. Although..."

"Oh no," I say.

"You said you took dance classes," she points out.

"It was six years ago. And I've had a kid since then." I poke my soft belly. "I have stretch marks now."

"We can cover those up," she scoffs. She gestures at the phone. "Mr. Thompson, the owner of the club, has asked for you."

"What do you mean? I don't know him."

"He saw you help Katie."

My eyebrows rise. "He was the guy with the mask?"

She nods. "He wants to know if you'll take her place."

My mouth forms an O. "But... I don't have any clothes..."

"We keep outfits here. You're tiny, and we'll definitely have something to fit you."

Me? A dancer? I start laughing. "No, that's ridiculous, I couldn't possibly..."

"We'll pay you a hundred pounds an hour," she says.

My smile fades. The job in the kitchen would have paid ten pounds an hour. I was supposed to work from seven until midnight, so I'd have earned fifty pounds in total.

"How long would I have to dance for?" I ask.

"Our dancers usually perform twenty minutes on, then have a twenty minute break, but we pay for the whole hour. If you could make it until midnight, that would be great."

Five hundred pounds instead of fifty. Oh my God.

I think about getting up on stage, dressed in a skimpy outfit, and dancing in front of an audience, presumably composed mainly of men, and a shiver runs down my back.

"Would I have to strip?" I ask.

Miranda shakes her head. "This is a very exclusive club, very classy. No nudity. The girls aren't allowed to harass the customers for private dances, but if the customer requests one, that's fine. Absolutely no touching, though. We're very strict about that."

I think about the fact that my rent is due on Boxing Day. That my festive food cupboard currently contains a jar of cranberry sauce and a box of Jacob's crackers. That the only presents I've been able to buy for Immi are a pack of coloring pencils and a Barbie from Oxfam. I've been unpicking old sweaters and using the wool to knit clothes for the doll at night when Immi has gone to bed, but I can only do basic patterns. She'd love the new Fashion Boutique playset.

More than that, I'm sure she'd love a roof over her head and something for dinner other than baked beans on toast for the hundredth time this year.

Carpe diem, right?

I can't wait to tell my best friend, Cora. She's going to crack a rib laughing.

"I'll do it," I say.

Miranda nods and tells the person at the other end of the phone, "She says yes." She listens again, and then her lips curve up. "Yes, sir, will do." She ends the call, and her gaze skims down me with renewed interest. She doesn't elaborate, though. Instead, she says, "Thank you for helping us out, we do appreciate it."

As we walk across the foyer, I say, "Mr. Thompson—was he in an accident or something?"

"A plane crash. It caught fire. He was badly burned." She opens the door and walks in. "Come on."

I go into a long room that looks like a changing room right out of a movie. Tables line the walls with large mirrors surrounded by bright bulbs. Several girls are in the process of doing their makeup and hair, while a couple of others are getting dressed. One takes off her bra right in front of me without batting an eyelid. I take some consolation from the fact that my boobs are bigger than hers.

"Here you go." Miranda gestures to one of the tables, and I take off my coat and hang it over the chair. "Now, let's get you kitted out."

She chooses me a red and gold sequined cropped top and the shortest shorts I've ever seen. She adds a matching pair of gloves I really like. They don't have fingers but instead a loop that slips over my middle finger to keep them in place, and they reach up to my elbows. She suggests I take out my butterfly clip and leave my long blonde hair loose. The girls bring their own makeup, but she finds a new pot of glittery gold eyeshadow that I smooth over my eyelids, and some dark-pink lip gloss. Finally she holds up a pair of gold shoes with, like, a five-inch wedge.

"Only if you want another rolled ankle," I state.

"You have tiny feet," she complains. "What about these?" She takes out a pair of shiny red sandals with a three-inch stiletto heel.

"I can't," I tell her. "I'll fall flat on my face. It's barefoot or nothing."

"Well, some guys like that," she says, amused.

I can barely believe my reflection. In less than fifteen minutes, I've turned from frumpy mum to sultry dancer. Well, almost. I turn from side to side, conscious of my generous curves. "I'm not used to exposing these to the public," I tell Miranda doubtfully.

"You look terrific," she says. "Not every man likes 'em skinny. Come on."

She leads the way out of the changing room, across the foyer, and up the staircase, which sweeps around and heads for a pair of double doors.

"Mr. Thompson has requested that you take stage E," Miranda says as she pulls open one of the doors. "That's the one nearest the VIP area. You must have really caught his eye." She gives me an amused look and heads into the club.

My retort vanishes as the sight, sound, and smell of the club overwhelms my senses. It's semi-dark, although the girls dancing on the five individual stages are each lit by a spotlight. The furnishings are midnight blue with lots of mirrors and chrome. On the back wall, behind the DJ, is a huge clock. Tables sit in sheltered nooks around a central dance floor. Several Christmas trees contain elegant blue and silver decorations, making me give a rueful smile as I think of our tree at home with its mismatched baubles and tinsel bought over the years.

The customers in the nooks, at the bar, and on the dance floor look as if they've stepped straight off a movie set. The women are all thin and beautiful, and they're all wearing expensive gowns, their hair is coiffured, and diamonds sparkle in their ears and on their fingers. The men all look like James Bond. I've never felt more intimidated in my life. What the hell am I doing here?

Miranda takes my hand and leads me through the crowd standing in front of the bar who are all cheering as one of the bartenders makes a cocktail à la Tom Cruise, spinning the shaker and pouring the ingredients from several feet high.

She heads for the small stage in the left-hand corner of the club. As we approach, I can see that the area is cordoned off with another bouncer standing in front, so clearly it's invitation-only. The bouncer nods at Miranda, lifts the hook to remove the rope, and lets us through before replacing it.

The VIP area consists of a series of private nooks, most of which are occupied by five or six people seated around a table. I spot a top footballer, a famous model, and a prominent politician, and try not to stare at an actor I saw in a movie last week.

The last nook is in the corner of the room, on a kind of raised dais so it has a good view of the entire room, but it's not lit, so the area remains in shadow. Miranda approaches the one person seated at the table. It's the man from her office. He's still wearing the hoodie, and the hood covers his hair and most of his face.

"Mr. Thompson," she says, stopping before him, "this is Astrid Bergman, who has very kindly offered to fill in for Katie tonight. Astrid, this is Te Ariki Thompson, owner of the Midnight Club."

Chapter Two

Te Ariki

"Thank you," I say to Miranda. "You can go."

She nods, glances at the blonde standing next to her, then walks away.

Astrid Bergman watches her leave, then eventually brings her gaze back to me. Slowly, I move the hood back a little.

People have all kinds of reactions when they meet me. Some spend the whole time looking at my chest or my feet, as if one glimpse at my face might turn them to stone. Others stare, unable to look away, clearly fascinated by the mask and what might lie beneath it.

Astrid does neither. She studies me calmly, although she's breathing fast, her chest rising and falling swiftly beneath the glittering red-and-gold top. Miranda has done a good job on her. Gone are the jeans, the awful sweater, the jacket that was two sizes too big for her, and the scruffy black boots. Her hair falls almost to her waist like a golden curtain, straight except for a slight kink where it had been held back with a clip. Her eyes look dark beneath the gold glitter on her lids, although downstairs I could have sworn they were blue. Her lips shine in the flashing lights from the dance floor.

She's average height, maybe 5'5", but she seems small in her bare feet. I heard her say that she has a child, and sure enough she's not as slender or toned as most of the other dancers. Instead she has C cup breasts, and her tummy is a soft curve above her tiny shorts.

She's also barefoot, and her neat toenails are bare of polish. I don't think I've ever seen one of my dancers without at least three-inch heels.

I lift my gaze to hers. Her cheeks bear a slight flush at my casual appraisal.

"Thank you for agreeing to cover for Katie," I say.

"You might end up regretting it," she replies. "I'm not as fit as I used to be. I hope you have an oxygen tank on standby."

That makes me give a short laugh. Her eyebrows rise, as if she hadn't considered that I might have a sense of humor.

"Te Ariki," she says. She pronounces it properly, the 'r' a quick tap of her tongue tip against the roof of her mouth. "You're Māori?" She pronounces that right, too, Mah-aw-ri, not rhyming the first syllable with 'cow' like most non-Kiwis do.

"Yes."

"*Meri Kirihimete*," she says. It means Merry Christmas. Her lips curve up. "I have a friend who was born in New Zealand."

I don't reply, more because I'm surprised than anything else. She lifts a hand to tuck her hair behind her ear, and the light catches her wedding ring.

"Won't your husband mind you dancing in a nightclub for the evening?" I ask. "Or are you not going to tell him?"

"I'm a widow," she replies. "But he wouldn't have cared if it meant I was earning money to buy our little girl some Christmas presents."

I'm shocked—she can only be in her early twenties. It's very young to be married and a mother, let alone to be a widow.

But then I, of all people, know how fragile that barrier is between life and death. And how easy it is to cross it, no matter what age you are.

"How did he die?" I ask.

She looks at her hands for a moment. Then she lifts her gaze to mine and says, "He killed himself."

I feel a sweep of pity for her. "I'm sorry to hear that."

We survey each other for a moment. Astrid returns my gaze calmly for about ten seconds, which is more than most, unnerving me, before she eventually looks away, over her shoulder, at the stage. I watch her moisten her lips with the tip of her tongue.

"Well," she says, "I suppose I should get started."

I give a curt nod.

She makes her way down the steps, out of the VIP area, and across to the small stage.

A waiter comes in with a glass on a tray, puts it before me, and leaves. I sip the thirty-year-old Macallan with a splash of water over ice, watching Astrid as she climbs the steps to the stage and approaches the pole. She glances over at me, then at the other VIP tables, gives a small sigh, then starts dancing.

I stretch out one arm along the back of the bench, prop my feet on a chair, and settle down to watch her.

From the start, it's clear that she doesn't have the experience of the other dancers in the club. Some of them have developed expert routines, and they've learned to climb the pole and perform an almost gymnastic sequence.

Despite her inexperience, Astrid moves with a sensual grace that makes my pulse gradually pick up speed. She moves to the thrumming beat of the music, circling her hips and shoulders, bending and straightening. The girl knows how to move, and there's something incredibly sexy about the fact that she's barefoot. At first she focuses her attention on the rest of the room, but she keeps glancing over at me, and eventually she turns and keeps her gaze fixed on me, as if she's dancing just for me. She uses the pole not just for support, but as the focus of her performance. It becomes a giant phallic symbol that she strokes and worships. By the time her twenty minutes comes to an end, my heart is pumping as fast as the music.

She disappears, presumably back downstairs for her break, then reappears and carries out her second performance. Once again she strokes, gyrates around, and makes love to the pole, and she receives a big cheer when she eventually finishes.

She continues like this for the next few hours. When she's on her breaks, I open my laptop and work. When she's performing, I pretend to work, but I spend most of the time watching Astrid. It's impossible to take my eyes off her. She fascinates me, I have no idea why.

By eleven thirty, her skin is covered with a sheen of sweat, and she's moving slower than before. If she's not used to dancing, no doubt her muscles are protesting. I wait until she's looking at me, then lift a hand and beckon.

She slows and stops, clearly puzzled, so I do it again. I watch her suck her bottom lip, and then she descends the steps and crosses the floor to the VIP area. She makes her way to my table and stands before me. Her skin shines in the lights from the nearby Christmas tree. She's breathing hard.

"Come and sit down for a minute," I tell her.

She looks at the chair. "It's okay, I'll be taking a break in a few minutes."

"You're exhausted. Sit down before you fall down."

Her cheeks, which are already flushed, redden even more. "I told Miranda that I was unfit," she snaps. "I haven't done this in years."

"It was an observation, not a criticism. Please, sit and have a drink with me." I gesture at the bottle of still water on the table. She glances at it, then picks it up, unscrews the lid, and drinks a quarter of it while she lowers herself into the chair.

"For a moment, when I bent down, I didn't think I'd get up again," she admits. She pauses, then her lips curve up. "Did you just laugh?"

"No." I beckon to the waiter, who comes over. "Would you like something stronger?" I ask her. "Maybe a glass of Champagne?"

She stares at me. "Um…"

I give a small smile and nod at the waiter, and he walks away.

I lean back again, one arm stretched out along the back of the chair. "You dance well," I tell her.

She blows a raspberry. "I don't, but thank you for saying so."

"I don't say things I don't mean."

"I have eyes. I was watching some of the other girls. If I got my leg half as high as some of them, I'd pull a hamstring. I'm incredibly unfit."

Again, I try not to laugh. "Maybe. But you're very graceful, and you move with a sensualness most of the others don't match."

She lifts her eyes to mine for a moment, then drops her gaze to her hands and fiddles with her nails. She's not sure whether to believe the compliment.

We sit quietly for a moment, listening to the music. I wonder whether she's going to feel awkward at the extended silence, but she spends the time glancing around the room, watching the crowd and the other dancers. The fairy lights make her eyes sparkle.

"I saw you rush to help Katie when she fell," I tell her.

She looks at me, surprised. "Oh. I thought you'd gone back upstairs."

I wasn't sure if she'd seen me in Miranda's office, but she obviously had. "You were very kind to her," I comment.

"I only did what everyone else would have done."

"No, you didn't. There are lots of people who would have either looked the other way or just stood there and watched the scene."

"Well, usually it's me falling down the stairs, so I know how it feels to be in that situation."

"You empathized."

"Yeah, I guess."

The waiter comes back with a tall glass of Champagne. He places it before Astrid, then leaves. She picks up the glass and sips it. "Nice," she says.

I smile. It's Dom Pérignon, and it costs over a thousand pounds a bottle. Clearly, she has no idea.

"Tell me about yourself," I say, because it seems polite to ask.

She moistens her lips with the tip of her tongue. "What do you want to know?"

"You said you have a child?"

"A little girl, yes. She's six."

"Is she looking forward to Christmas?"

"Yes. I'm busy making as many doll's clothes as I can before Christmas Day." She studies her Champagne, then has a sip.

She's already mentioned that she can't afford to buy presents for the girl. I think about how I can happily throw away a thousand pounds on a bottle of Champagne or a few hundred thousand on another car when I already have five in my garage. We're worlds apart, and we have nothing in common.

So why does she fascinate me?

"Where are you from in New Zealand?" she asks.

I'm taken aback by the question. "A coastal city called Tauranga in the Bay of Plenty."

"How long have you been in the UK?"

"Two years. I run the European branch of the family business." I speak curtly; I don't want to talk about myself. In fact, I don't really want to talk at all. I don't want to know more about her and how she can't afford to buy her little girl presents. That's not why I asked her here.

"I have a proposition for you," I say.

"Oh?"

"I'd like you to give me a private dance."

She stares at me for about twenty seconds. I return her gaze steadily.

In the end, she says, "What?" The expression on her face is almost comical.

I don't repeat my statement. I sip my whisky and wait for her reply.

"A lap dance?" she says eventually.

"If you like."

Her mouth opens to reply, but no words come out.

She swallows. "I don't know…"

"I'll pay you five thousand pounds." I pluck the amount out of the air, picking a figure I think is likely to convince her.

Her eyes widen. "What?"

It's impossible not to let my lips curve up, just a little.

"Five thousand?" she asks incredulously.

I nod.

"I don't understand," she says. "I'm no good at this. I'm not an expert. I'm just me."

"Is that a no?"

A frown flickers on her brow. "Are you serious?"

"Yes."

"Why? I mean, why do you want *me* to dance for you?"

I don't reply.

"Are you making fun of me?" she asks.

It's my turn to frown. "No. Why would you think that?"

"I just don't understand. There are loads of gorgeous girls out there who know exactly how to do it."

"But I want you," I reply.

She stares at me again. Her blue eyes are very big and sparkly in the fairy lights.

"What would I have to do?" Her voice is a whisper, and I can hardly hear it above the music.

"Just dance."

"Here?"

"Yes."

"Do I have to touch you?"

"That's up to you. But customers aren't allowed to touch the dancers."

"Do I have to take off my clothes?"

"No."

"But it's supposed to be an erotic dance, right?

"Yes."

We study each other for a moment. She's breathing fast, clearly nervous.

"You're under no obligation," I say eventually. "I'm sure Miranda has taken your bank account details?" She nods. "She will already have organized payment for this evening," I continue.

"But you'll pay me another five thousand pounds if I dance just for you?"

"Yes."

"Are you crazy?"

"Maybe." The light from behind her gives her blonde hair a halo. "You look like an angel." I don't even realize I've spoken until her eyebrows lift.

"I'm not," she says. "Far from it."

"Better and better."

She gives a short laugh, and for the first time, a mischievous glint appears in her eyes. "All right."

I'm surprised. I thought she was going to refuse. She knocks back the last mouthful of Champagne and says, "Dutch courage," and then my pulse picks up speed as she rises from the chair.

The VIP nooks don't have doors as such, but they do have curtains that can be used for privacy. Without asking, Astrid pulls our curtain across, enclosing us in our own private lair.

On the table, a candle flickers in the middle of a tinsel decoration, while the fairy lights that run along the top of the nook sparkle, providing the only light as she turns to face me. I shift along the bench a little so I'm free of the table, then rest my arms on the back and stretch out my legs, crossing them at the ankles.

She chews her bottom lip. "If I'm rubbish, you don't have to pay me," she says.

I just meet her gaze, not saying anything. I already know she's going to be amazing.

She inhales and lets the breath out slowly. The music is loud, the base thudding up through the floor, into my bones.

Astrid starts to dance.

At first, she moves self-consciously; clearly the thought of doing a private performance is very different for her from dancing on the stage. She starts in front of me, moving to the beat, winding her hips as she lowers down and then puts her hands on her knees and pushes up.

"Hopefully you can't hear my knees crack," she says. "It's not the sexiest sound."

That makes me give a short laugh, and it seems to relax her a bit, because she flashes me a smile and moves closer to me. I have a sip of whisky, more to give myself something to do with my hands, as she stands either side of my outstretched legs and dances.

Slowly, possibly due to the Dom Pérignon working its magic, she grows more confident. She keeps her gaze fixed on my face, and gradually, in time to the music, she moves closer to me, until her knees are touching the front of the bench.

Bending forward, she rests on the back, on either side of my shoulders, and leans in close. She looks into my eyes and moistens her lips with the tip of her tongue.

"How am I doing?" she asks, her voice a tad husky.

I don't answer, but I do keep my gaze on hers.

Her lips curve up a fraction. As if she's taken on an unspoken challenge, she leans closer to me until her lips just brush mine. She stays there for a moment, and I hold my breath, wondering if she's going to kiss me, but then she moves up, arching her back sensually, so her chest passes in front of my face before she straightens. The red-and-gold cropped top is Christmassy and sexy, and it clings to her breasts and gives her a generous cleavage. Miranda must have given her some body glitter, because her neck and breasts bear an attractive shine as they catch the sparkle of the fairy lights.

I uncross my feet and bring them closer to me, and she lowers down so she's sitting on my thighs, close to my knees, and dances to the music there for a while. She might not have done this professionally before, but she's obviously picked up some tricks from the few classes she's taken, or maybe it's just natural talent that's making her move so sensually. I keep my arms along the back of the bench, even though I'm tempted to touch her, drawn by the flare of her hips, the curve of her waist, and the swell of her breasts.

After a while, she lifts up and turns so she's facing away from me, then lowers down again onto my thighs, rocking her hips suggestively, and gradually getting closer to me, until finally her back meets my chest. I keep my arms stretched out, not touching her as she circles her hips, pressing back against me.

Abruptly, she freezes, waits a moment, and then looks over her shoulder at me.

She swallows hard. "Do you want me to stop?"

She's felt my erection.

"No," I reply.

Her gaze meets mine. I can feel the heat of her body against me, even through my suit. It would be so easy to kiss her bare shoulder, all the way up her neck to her jaw, her cheek, and finally her mouth. I want to feel how soft her skin is; I want to feel her lips beneath mine. Her gaze drops to my mouth, and I know then that she's thinking about kissing me.

But I remain still, and eventually she lifts up and turns to face me again, lowering down so she's resting on my thighs. This time, she slides further up them so we're an inch apart. She undoes the buttons on my jacket and pushes the sides apart.

"I like the silver swirls on this," she murmurs, touching my bow tie.

"They're called korus," I mumble. "It's the shape of a newly unfurling silver fern. I have the ties imported from Christchurch in New Zealand." Conscious I'm waffling, I stop talking as she begins to move to the music again.

She rocks her hips, rolling her shoulders, and winding her body in a way that makes my heart race.

Resting her hands on the back of the bench, she leans in close to me, keeping her mouth a fraction of an inch from mine. I can feel the heat of her body through my shirt. Her breath whispers across my lips, sending the hairs rising on the back of my neck.

My hands tighten into fists as she continues to writhe on top of me. This is backfiring on me big time. She drops her head as if she's about to kiss me, her shining lips parting, and I imagine her soft tongue sliding against mine, her teeth tugging lightly on my bottom lip. As she rocks her hips again, she leans against me, pressing her breasts to my chest.

I want to slip my hands into her top, cup her breasts with my palms, and tease her nipples with my thumbs. I want to cover them with my mouth, suck them and tug them with my teeth. I want to brush my hands up her silky thighs and into her shorts and discover whether she's wet and swollen and ready for me. I want to slide inside her, and thrust us both to a magnificent climax.

Abruptly, lowering an arm around her waist, I get to my feet. Astrid gasps and tightens her legs around my waist, clutching hold of my shoulders. I stand there, fighting the urge to carry her out through my private doorway, take her upstairs to my room, toss her on the bed, and make love to her until she cries out my name.

But her eyes are wide with panic. I paid her to dance for me tonight, and the likelihood is that if I ask her to come with me, she'll say no and run from the club so fast she'll leave scorch marks on the midnight-blue carpet.

Slowly, I lower her, and she slides down me until her feet touch the floor. With both hands on her hips, I move her a foot away from me.

I take out my phone, pull up my banking app, and bring up the club accounts. Miranda has already added Astrid, and it takes seconds to transfer the five thousand pounds into her account.

"I've paid you," I say gruffly, pocketing my phone. "You can go now."

She stares up at me. Fuck me, she's beautiful, her hair glowing around her head like a halo, her blue eyes shining in the candlelight.

"You want me to finish on the stage?" she asks. "It's not twelve yet."

Even as she speaks, though, the clock on the wall strikes midnight, the sound ringing through the club like Big Ben. The crowd on the dance floor cheers as silver glitter flutters down from above them like snowflakes.

"You can go," I say. I sit down and toss back the last mouthful of whisky in my glass. Astrid opens the curtain, and I wait for her to walk out.

She hesitates, though. "Thank you for the work tonight," she says softly. "The money will make a big difference to me and my daughter. I really appreciate it—it was very generous of you considering I had no idea what I was doing, and I'm sure I was terrible at it."

Her magnanimous comment is the last thing I'm expecting, and my jaw drops. Before I can reply and reassure her how amazing she was, she runs down the steps and pushes through the crowd, heading for the doors to the ground floor.

I sit there, full of frustration, confused and vexed, and with no outlet for the desire that's raging inside me.

Chapter Three

Astrid

It's Immi's last day at school, and everyone in the class is supposed to bring a plate of food to share at lunchtime. Because I was out working last night, my mum made fairy cakes with her, which Immi is now carrying in a tin on her lap as I push her wheelchair into the school grounds.

She's super excited, and I smile as I take her into her classroom, where Vicky, the teaching assistant, takes over.

"See you later," I promise Immi, and she flings her arms around my neck and hugs me before she goes off with Vicky to put her tin on the lunch table with the others.

I leave the classroom and head outside into the cold morning. Flakes of snow flutter around my head, but they've yet to thicken and start laying.

Stretching my arms over my head, I groan as my muscles protest. Talk about a workout last night. Gosh, I'm unfit. I really need to think about an exercise regime going into the New Year.

I cross the road, heading for the law firm where I'm going to be temping for the next few days. I know a lot of people dislike temping, and it's true that it would be nice to have a secure job and a regular wage, but I quite like going to different firms each week, and never knowing what job I'm going to be doing until I turn up.

Last night was completely unexpected, though. I can't help a short laugh as I think about what I ended up doing. I didn't have the courage to tell Mum when I got home, although I did text my best friend, Cora, earlier this morning, prompting a flurry of texts with more than the usual amount of exclamation marks as she demanded to know more details.

When my phone buzzes in my pocket, I assume it's her with another barrage of questions, but the screen reads 'unknown caller'.

I answer it as I wait at the crossing. "Hello?"

"Astrid? It's Miranda Clark, from Midnight in Mayfair."

My eyebrows shoot up. "Oh. Hello!"

"Good morning. Is this a convenient moment?"

Someone bumps into me, and I hurriedly join the crowd crossing the road. "Yes, I'm on my way to a job."

"Okay, I'll be quick anyway. I wondered if you were available tonight?"

"You mean to work in the kitchen?"

She laughs. "No, as a dancer."

"Seriously? Mr. Thompson sent me away last night. I assumed I sucked." I realize how that sounds and quickly add, "At the dancing, I mean."

She chuckles. "Well, you must have done something right because he's personally requested you for the rest of the week."

Te Ariki has requested me? My mouth goes completely dry as I think about last night, and how he asked me to give him a personal dance. How I sat astride his legs and moved against him, and how I felt his erection, which seemed like an obvious indicator of his desire for me. How I felt his breathing speed up, and the warmth of his body through his shirt when I undid his jacket. The smell of his cologne—I don't know much about expensive scents, but it smelled of both sandalwood and blackcurrant, and it was deeply seductive. How his breath whispered across my lips, and how, even though he scared me, I wanted to kiss him.

Then I remember the moment he grasped me around the waist, picked me up, unceremoniously dumped me on the floor, and snapped at me to leave. He was so intimidating, tall and big and menacing with the face mask and the hood pulled over his head, and it took every ounce of courage I possessed not to just bolt from the room. The last thing I want to do is go back to the club, stand in front of him, and dance for him again.

But then I think about the money. Five hundred pounds a night, for the rest of the week? I can't afford to turn that down.

"Y-yes," I stammer. "Of... of course. Seven until midnight?"

"Yes, please. Okay, we'll see you then. Have a great day."

"You too." But she's already hung up.

I slide the phone back into my pocket, my head spinning. Last night, even though it was late by the time I got home, I stayed awake for an hour in bed, thinking about the events of the evening, and wondering what I did wrong, and why he snapped at me. In the end, I just assumed I'd bored him. But that obviously wasn't the case.

I'm on the reception desk at the law firm, and I'm kept busy until lunchtime, when everyone disappears to a local restaurant for the office party. Apart from answering the occasional phone call and taking messages, it's just me for over an hour, and I spent the time on my phone, Googling Te Ariki Thompson.

I'm fascinated by what I find. He actually has a Wikipedia page! It describes him as a New Zealand media executive, and the eldest son of Aaron Thompson, who is the creator and chief executive officer of The Thompson Company, which is a multinational mass media and entertainment conglomerate. I've heard of Thompsons, of course, but I hadn't put two and two together. It explains how Aaron Thompson's incredible business acumen led to him building up a billion-dollar business over thirty years. I have to stop and think about that for a moment. Does that mean Te Ariki is a billionaire? I Google that too—it's a thousand million. Nine noughts! Holy shit. I can't even conceive of that kind of money. I think about the twenty-six pounds fifty-two pence that was in my bank account until yesterday, and laugh out loud.

Te Ariki is the Managing Director of the European branch of Thompsons. The article goes into detail about his qualifications—so many letters—and his business achievements, but I scroll down to read the stuff that's more interesting to me. He has a majority stake in Crystal Palace Football Club here in London, and he also a supporter of a Kiwi company that coaches youngsters in rugby. He's the patron of several big charities and has raised money for them personally by running charity balls and silent auctions held at Midnight in Mayfair.

I read about the club with interest. Three years ago, while he was still in New Zealand, he began a company called Midnight with a group of his close friends. They created a series of private members' clubs across New Zealand—and now in England—which function during the day as places to gather with like-minded people to do business and to socialize, and at nighttime, as exclusive nightclubs. But the article speculates that the Midnight Clubs are pretty much just a front for this group of altruistic billionaires who very quietly and privately donate a significant amount of money to charities and other important international causes.

Hmm.

I scroll down to his personal details, feeling a little like I'm spying, but powerless to stop. Te Ariki is twenty-eight, and he grew up on Aaron's million-dollar estate in New Zealand. There's a picture of it. Wow. It looks like Buckingham Palace. He's been living in England for the past two years. I stare at the photo of him that was taken before his accident on Christmas Eve last year. He's gorgeous, with light-brown skin, thick dark hair cut in a fashionable fade, and startling chocolate-brown eyes.

Aaahhh… now I remember reading about him. I thought I recalled his name. He used to be quite the socialite. Both in New Zealand and the UK he was linked with lots of beautiful women—models and actresses—gaining quite the reputation of a Casanova/James Bond, and he was one of the most eligible bachelors in London. But that all went wrong a year ago.

With a thudding heart, I read about the accident. He has a pilot's license, and last Christmas Eve, he was flying his younger brother back to London from a trip to Scotland when something went wrong with the landing gear, and the plane crashed and burst into flames. A friend who was waiting for them at the airport dragged them out of the wreckage, but not before the fire had burned a good portion of the left side of Te Ariki's face, neck, and body. His brother died at the scene.

There's a picture of Te Ariki with his last girlfriend, a beautiful actress called Sara May, but they broke up shortly after the accident. I frown as I read about how society turned on him afterwards, how journalists camped outside the club to try to catch a sight of the masked Te Ariki, and how they reported gleefully that the arrogant billionaire had been brought down a peg or two, implying that he deserved everything he got, and how the mighty have fallen.

The article states he's now single and lives almost as a recluse, running his business from his luxury penthouse above Midnight in Mayfair that overlooks Green Park. Ohhh… I'm beginning to understand why he sits in the corner in the shadows on his own…

I feel a sweep of sorrow as I think about the photo of the gorgeous guy with the beautiful actress on his arm, and the broken man I met last night, with his mask and hood, who was clearly ashamed and embarrassed about his wounds and scars.

The article states he's 'confident, charming, and charismatic.' Those wouldn't be the words I'd choose to describe him. The accident obviously changed him in ways other than physically.

I spend the rest of the day with a racing heart every time I think about what's going to happen this evening. At five thirty, I rush to pick up Immi from her after-school club because Mum is working tonight and can't meet me until just after seven. I've texted Miranda to say I might be five minutes late, and she said that was fine. I find some spaghetti Bolognese I made previously in bulk and froze, defrost two portions, dish them up for me and Immi, and we sit and eat them while Immi tells me about her Christmas party. Afterward, I make sure she's comfortable in front of the TV watching *Frozen* for the bajillionth time, then head to my bedroom and get ready.

Tonight, I make more of an effort on my appearance than I did yesterday. Not for Te Ariki, but because… hell, who am I kidding? It's totally for Te Ariki, because I want him to ask me to dance for him personally again. Well, I'd be stupid not to want an extra five thousand pounds, right?

Then, as the water heats up in the shower, I stare at my reflection, feeling a stab of guilt. He must be overwhelmed by people who are only interested in his money. As much as I'm desperate for cash, I don't like the thought of dancing for him only for his money.

So what does that mean? Why else would I dance for him?

I think about the heat from his body as I pressed against him, and the way he dropped his gaze to my mouth as if he was thinking about kissing me. Despite the fact that he was intimidating, and that with the hood up he looked nothing like his photo on Wikipedia, I still found him attractive. And when he almost laughed as I joked about my knees cracking, I saw a glimpse of the man he had been, and I liked him.

But that's just silly. This is purely physical. There could never be anything between us. We're like planets in the solar system, circling the sun but never meeting one another, existing in different orbits. I don't understand his world, and he doesn't understand mine. No, this is purely about money. About Immi, and what this will mean for her. I'll be able to have some really nice food for Christmas, and a proper stocking of presents. I can treat us both to some new clothes rather than having to continually mend old ones until they're more darning than fabric. And I'll actually be able to have a few pounds in the bank. That's all this is about.

So I shower and blow-dry my hair, although I leave it down as Te Ariki seemed to like it, and I put on some makeup, using black eyeliner to create the winged cat-eye look, with sparkly eyeshadow, and paint my lips dark pink.

When I come out, Immi's eyes widen. "It's very Christmassy there," I tell her. "I thought I'd add a bit of sparkle."

"You'll be the prettiest person in the kitchen," she says.

I blush. "Um… yes, hopefully."

She picks up the item sitting on the table next to her coloring pencils and holds it out to me. "You should wear this."

I look at it and laugh. It's a headband with a hoop above it wrapped in tinsel.

You look like an angel.

I'm not. Far from it.

Better and better.

"All right," I say mischievously. I slot the band onto my head and check it out in the mirror. The halo sits just above my hair, the gold tinsel glittering in the light.

"Come on," I tell her. "We'd better get going."

I help her on with her coat, lift her into her wheelchair, and call an Uber. The bus and the Tube would be cheaper, but it's such a hassle with her wheelchair, and besides, I've got five thousand five hundred pounds in my bank account tonight, so I feel in the mood to treat us.

The Uber driver stays sitting in his car, leaving it up to me to lift Immi into the back and then put the wheelchair into the boot, knocking my halo in the process. I mumble under my breath as I get in beside Immi.

Fifteen minutes later, we pull up outside the club. I try to ignore the line of customers waiting to go in as I struggle to get the wheelchair out. It refuses to come, and I realize it's hooked on something inside the boot. Nobody comes to help, and I curse under my breath as I try to unhook it.

I'm just about to yell at the waiting customers and ask whether they have any Christmas spirit left in their expensive leather wallets when Carl runs up.

"Here you go," he says, unsnagging the wheelchair and removing it from the car. He opens it while I lift Immi into it, both of us shivering in the cool evening air.

"Thank you so much," I say gratefully as I make sure she's comfortable. "How did you see us from the alley?"

"Mr. Thompson called me," he says, gesturing up. I look up just in time to see a dark figure at the window on the next floor before he disappears.

"Oh. Well, thank you anyway, I really appreciate your help."

"No worries at all."

"Astrid!"

I turn to see my mother approaching and give her a big smile. "Hey, Mum. Um… this is Carl, he works here. Carl, this is my mum."

"Hello, Carl," Mum says, shaking his hand. "I'm so sorry I'm late," she says to me, "I came as quickly as I could."

"No, you're fine." I know her cleaning job finishes at seven on the dot.

She looks at my halo, and then her gaze drops to my face, where she obviously notices my makeup. "You look nice," she says, amused.

"Christmas," I mumble, as if it explains everything.

Her lips twitch. "Come on," she says to Immi. "We'll let Mum get to work."

"Bye sweetie." I bend and give Immi a big hug. "Have fun." Mum's taking her to Oxford Street to see the Christmas lights there before they return to our flat in Camden.

I watch them walk away, then flash Carl a smile as we head to the back door.

"Pretty little girl," he says. "Like her mum."

"Aw." I nudge him. "Smooth talker."

He chuckles. "Have a great evening."

"See you later." I go into the club, relieved to be out of the bitter cold. I check in with Miranda, then head to the changing rooms. Within ten minutes, I've changed into a new cropped top and skimpy shorts covered in gold and blue sequins. I check my appearance briefly, then head out and up the stairs, and go through the double doors into the club.

Miranda has instructed me to head to stage E again, which is currently empty. As I approach it, I glance at the VIP area and see Te Ariki sitting at his table, alone, in shadow, his hood pulled over his head. He doesn't acknowledge my presence, so I don't know whether he's seen me or not. I swallow hard, climb the steps to the pole, and begin dancing.

My muscles protest, but I push through the stiffness, finding it easier once I've warmed up a bit. I like dancing, and I enjoy music with a heavy beat, and it doesn't take long for me to get into the swing of it. After a while, I forget about my aches and pains, and I forget about the crowds of people who barely seem to glance at me.

I work twenty minutes on, twenty off, all evening. I don't know how much of my performances Te Ariki catches; I'm sure I can feel his steady gaze on me, even though I can't see his eyes, but he has his laptop out, and occasionally he's on his phone, so maybe he hasn't even noticed I'm here. It's only when I approach the stage for the final time that he gestures for me to approach him.

My mouth going dry, I cross to the VIP area, and the bouncer lets me in. I walk past the other nooks to the one at the end and go inside.

Te Ariki is sitting on the bench, arms outstretched along the back. My heart bangs to the heavy beat of the music as I lower onto the chair in front of him.

"Good evening," he says.

"Evening." I moisten my lips.

He gestures at the stage. "Thank you for coming back tonight."

"You're welcome. I'm surprised you asked for me."

"Really?"

"I thought you were cross with me last night."

He doesn't reply to that. Instead, he lifts his gaze to my halo. "It's bent," he points out.

"No surprises there." I try to straighten it. He watches, his lips curving up a little.

I lower my hands, smiling as a waiter approaches with a glass of what I presume is Champagne. He hands it to me and withdraws, and I sip it while Te Ariki watches.

"This is getting to be a habit," I tell him.

He picks up his glass and has a mouthful of the amber liquid, then returns the glass to the table.

"Can you do me a favor?" I ask him. When his eyebrows lift, I say, "Can you lower your hood? I can't see your eyes."

He stares at me, and for a moment I think he's going to refuse, maybe even bark at me to leave. But after about ten seconds, he raises a hand, hesitates, then pushes the hood back.

The mask covers most of his forehead, all his nose, and the left side of his face, although his mouth appears untouched. His white shirt has a wing-tip collar that covers most of his neck, but I can just see a touch of puckered skin above it, beneath the bottom of the mask.

My heart races, but I look into his eyes, which are lit by the twinkling fairy lights.

"Your eyes are very expressive," I say. "You shouldn't hide them."

He has another mouthful of whisky, not replying. I sip my Champagne, mostly to give my hands something to do.

He doesn't say anything, so I glance around the club, lifting a hand to my lips to stifle a yawn.

"Are you tired?" he asks.

"Sorry. I've been temping at a law firm all day. Thank you for sending Carl to help me earlier, by the way. The wheelchair was hooked on something."

He nods. "She's your little girl?"

"Yes, Imogen—Immi. She has Spina Bifida. Do you know anything about it?"

"Not much, I'm ashamed to say."

"It's when the neural tube that develops into the spinal cord and brain doesn't close during pregnancy and leaves a gap in the spine."

"What causes it?"

"I didn't realize I was pregnant until the pregnancy was quite advanced, and so I didn't take folic acid supplements, which didn't help. But my husband's brother has it, so it's more likely to be genetic. She can't walk without help, and she has… other problems." My voice trails off before I mention her lack of bladder and bowel control as I realize how unromantic and unsexy this is. He didn't invite me here to talk about my disabled daughter.

But he says, "Is there treatment available?"

"She had orthopedic surgery a couple of times when she was a baby, but it wasn't as successful as we'd hoped. Now it's really about managing it—she has physical therapy a few times a week, and we're teaching her about skin care and how to monitor her own functions."

"It's a lot to cope with on your own."

"I have my mum. She lives with us, and she looks after Immi when I'm working. And I have quite a big family, aunts and uncles and cousins, and lots of friends who are willing to help."

"That must be nice."

His words imply he doesn't know what that's like. I think about the Wikipedia article that said he and his brother grew up on a huge estate in New Zealand. I wonder what his childhood was like?

"I read about you," I state. "On Wikipedia."

He glares at me. Ooh, he doesn't like that. His hand twitches, and it makes me think that he wants to pull up his hood, to hide away again, but he doesn't.

"And what fascinating facts did you dig up?" he asks sarcastically.

"Crystal Palace FC, seriously? You could at least have gone for Chelsea."

His lips curve up slowly, and then he laughs—a deep, husky chuckle that gives me goosebumps all over. "I have a friend who's a supporter," he admits. "He took me to see them when I first came here. Are you a soccer fan?"

"Soccer? Honestly," I scold, "you've been here long enough to call it football. Yes, I'm a fan, although I don't go much now, at fifty-five pounds a ticket."

He nods and glances at his phone. I assume he's checking a text or something, but then he says, "it's 11:45. You have fifteen minutes left. Are you going to dance for me again?"

My pulse immediately picks up speed. "Would you like me to?"

"If you'd like to."

I want to. I want to sit on his lap, undo the buttons of his jacket, and move up close to him again. I want to feel his erection pressing against me, and know it's me he wants. I want to look into his eyes and know he's thinking about me, and only me.

But that's ridiculous. This is all about money, right?

"How much will you pay me?" I ask.

As soon as I say it, I wince at the words. But he doesn't flinch. "Five thousand," he says, "same as yesterday."

"For fifteen minutes?"

He nods.

I push my guilt and embarrassment away and think about Immi. "Okay."

I knock back the rest of my Champagne and get to my feet. He shifts to the end of the bench, stretching out his arms again along the back.

I dance in front of him for about five minutes, my heart thudding as his eyes burn into me like lasers. He parts his legs, letting me dance between them, and, with my back to him, I lower myself onto his lap and rock my hips, circling my butt. He grunts his approval, so I do that for a bit longer, lifting my arms above my head and scooping up my hair so he can see my neck and the curve of my figure.

Finally, I turn, lift a leg over his so I'm kneeling on the bench either side of his hips, and lower onto his thighs.

He doesn't move, and when I look into his eyes, I find them studying my face. Keeping my gaze on his, I slide my hands down him to his jacket, unbutton it, and push the sides apart. Then I place both hands on his chest. The heat of his body sears through his shirt, and when I rest one hand over his heart, I can feel its rapid, rhythmic thud.

Slowly, I shift closer to him, sliding up his thighs. The song has changed to something slow and moody. Sure enough, he has an erection again, and I can't help but move to the music, rocking my hips against him.

I slide my hands up his chest, lowering my lips to just above his, and I feel him sigh. I wonder whether the Wikipedia article was right, and he hasn't dated since his accident. If so, he must be desperate to touch and be touched. Just like me.

I shouldn't. I mustn't.

I moisten my lips with the tip of my tongue. He watches, breathing fast, but he doesn't move.

"Can I kiss you?" I whisper.

He doesn't reply for a moment. I wait, my lips a fraction of an inch from his.

Then, eventually, he gives a slight nod.

My heart hammers, but I make myself stay calm as I lower my head.

I kiss him slowly, pressing my lips against his with light, unthreatening kisses that nevertheless make me breathless and dizzy with longing. I kiss from one corner of his mouth to the other, then back again, and finish in the center. Tilting my head to the right a little to change the angle, and closing my eyes, I touch the tip of my tongue to his bottom lip, requesting entrance. His lips part, and his tongue slides against mine, sensual and erotic.

I'm guessing that he doesn't want me to touch him anywhere near his mask, but I can't help lifting a hand to cup his right cheek. I want to touch his skin, and I find it warm, the bristles of his five o'clock shadow scraping against my thumb as I brush it over his cheek. I make sure to keep away from the mask, instead sliding my hand back a little to the nape of his neck, and feeling the short hair there.

I sigh, which comes out as a soft moan, and in response he lowers one arm around me and rests his hand flat against my back between my shoulder blades with a light pressure, keeping me in place. It's breaking the rules, a customer touching one of the dancers. But he owns the club, so I guess he gets special dispensation. I'm not about to complain, anyway.

We kiss like that for about five minutes, slowly, leisurely, and I think he's enjoying the contact as much as I am, the gentle exploration, the very essence of a kiss, which is about sharing yourself in the most intimate way with someone.

Eventually, he tightens his arm around my waist, gets to his feet, and lowers my legs to the floor. I slide down him, very aware of the hard bulge in his trousers.

We stand there like that for a moment, him looking down into my eyes. Then he takes a step back and picks up his phone. He taps a few times and says, "I've put the money into your account. Goodnight."

I clear my throat. "Um… 'night."

I hesitate for a second, wanting to say something that acknowledges the connection I feel we've just had. That explains how I feel right now.

But he sits back down and starts scrolling on his phone, and so I turn and walk away.

Chapter Four

Te Ariki

This close to Christmas, the club is heaving with businessmen and office types who've come here after their office parties to prolong the atmosphere and continue the romances most of them have been cultivating all day.

From my nook in the corner of the club, I watch the throng with distaste, wishing I could just close the club and send them all home. I much prefer being here during the day, when it's quiet and everyone's here to work. But the nightclub makes an extortionate amount of money, with a membership of over three thousand pounds a year, plus a table fee of a thousand pounds if a member decides to bring guests. You'd be amazed what people are willing to pay for exclusivity.

I don't feel bad about charging exorbitant prices though, because after paying the staff's wages and the costs of running Midnight, all profit made here goes to charity. Not that I'd feel guilty even if I pocketed all the profit. I've worked hard to get where I am, and I've paid a high price for my success.

"Hey." The man's voice jolts me out of my musings. "Stop brooding. You're like Bruce Wayne."

The other two men with him chuckle, and I give them a wry look. "I wasn't brooding. I was thinking."

These three businessmen are my co-founders of Midnight in Mayfair, and they're all Kiwis. Kingi Davis and Orson Cavendish are two of my oldest friends. I met them at our very expensive and exclusive private school, and although they reside mainly in New Zealand, they both have family in the UK, which means they travel here often.

Kingi is six-four and huge, with a personality to match. He plays rugby, cricket, and football—well, any type of sport, really. He's been off camping and rock climbing in the Peak District, which is why he currently has a thick bushy beard that we keep teasing him about.

Orson's the brains of the business, a financial wizard with an IQ of 161, who wouldn't be seen dead with any form of beard. He can be exceptionally dorky, but luckily he has the looks of a movie star and the dress sense of an Italian, and wears suits so sharp you could cut yourself on them, so he tends to get more female attention than the rest of us put together. I think it's more due to the fact that, even though he's only in his late twenties, his dark hair has a streak of gray at each temple, inherited from his father. Girls love gray hair, no idea why.

The other guy is called Lincoln Green. He insists he wasn't named after the color of Robin Hood's tights, but I'm not convinced. He's actually an archaeologist with an almost-supernatural talent for finding rare and valuable artifacts, and as a result he's made a fortune selling them to places like the British Museum. He's been over here about five years. I met him when I first came to the UK, and liked him immediately. We became good friends, and he was the one who was waiting for me and Hemi at the airport, and who pulled us out of the flames when we crashed. I owe him my life. He's a generous guy, and he was quick to jump on board when I suggested setting up a Midnight Club here.

"Difficult to tell the difference between brooding and thinking," he says. "They have the same glaring expression."

I pick up the bottle of twenty-six-year-old Glenfiddich Grand Couronne that cost me close to a thousand pounds and pour another inch into each of our glasses. "Drink up," I instruct. "You're nowhere close to being inebriated, and this is not the week for staying sober."

They know I'm not referring to the fact that it's nearly Christmas. Kingi picks up his glass and holds it out, and the rest of us do the same, clinking the crystal tumblers gently.

"To Hemi," Kingi says.

"To Hemi," we repeat, and have a mouthful of the whisky. It has a hint of spice and caramel, and it sears all the way down to my stomach.

"Fuck, that's good." Orson runs his tongue over his front teeth. "Wow."

"I bought five bottles," I tell him. "But it's not a patch on the bottle of Glenfiddich fifty-year-old Time Series. It's thirty thousand pounds a bottle."

Kingi whistles, and Orson laughs.

"I bet that's *smooth as*," Linc says.

"Like a woman's thighs," I reply, adding somewhat gloomily, "from what I recall."

Kingi gives me an amused look. "You need to get back out there, bro. You won't find Mrs. Right while you're holed up in here every night."

"I saw Sara yesterday," Linc says.

I have another mouthful of whisky, not replying.

"She asked after you," he adds.

"That was nice of her," Kingi says. His words drip with sarcasm.

"I told her to go fuck herself," Linc replies.

That makes me laugh. "You did not."

"No, I didn't," he admits, "but I wish I had. Two minutes after she walked away, I saw Ryan Lamb rest his hand on her arse."

We all snort. Ryan Lamb has dated every single woman in the whole of London.

"He's welcome to her," I say bitterly.

I don't tell them that I still get regular calls from Sara, begging me to take her back again. Unbidden, my brain flashes up a memory of the moment she came into the hospital and first saw me after the accident. I'll never forget the revulsion on her face before she did her best to swiftly wipe it away. Like most women I meet, she wants the money first and me second.

"Pretty girl," Linc says.

"Not in spirit," I reply.

"Not Sara," he says. "The dancer." He gestures at the nearby stage.

My head snaps around. I'd lost track of time—it's gone seven. The stage is occupied by the small, curvy form of the blonde angel who's occupied my thoughts almost continuously since I first set eyes on her three days ago.

"What's her name?" Kingi asks.

"Angel," I say. Then I realize what I've said. Shit. "I mean Astrid."

The three of them immediately look interested. "You've spoken to her?" Orson asks.

"She works for me," I reply. "I do occasionally talk to the staff."

"Why did you call her angel?" Kingi asks.

I glance over at her. She's not wearing the fake halo tonight, but the bright light behind her makes her blonde hair gleam.

"Never mind," he says, following my gaze. "Answered my own question."

She's dancing now, winding her body up and down the pole with the sensual grace that fascinates me so much. Tonight she's wearing a bright-red sequined cropped top and shorts so tight that they leave nothing to the imagination. I watch her lower to her haunches, then push up, and remember her saying, *Hopefully you can't hear my knees crack. It's not the sexiest sound.* The memory makes me chuckle.

"She's wearing a wedding ring," Linc observes.

"Her husband died," I say, reluctant to admit I know these personal details about her.

"She can only be in her early twenties," Orson comments.

"How did he die?" Linc asks.

"He killed himself."

"Jesus," he says.

"I'm guessing she didn't get any insurance money because of that," Orson says.

My eyebrows lift. "I hadn't thought of that."

"Why did he kill himself?" Linc asks.

"I don't know. I haven't asked her."

We all fall silent, and I'm sure they're all thinking as I am, about how bad you have to feel to take that final step.

"She came here on Monday to work in the kitchen," I say eventually, "but we were short of dancers, and she admitted she'd taken a few classes when she was younger, so Miranda asked her if she'd fill in for us."

"That was brave of her," Linc says.

"I think she needs the money. She has a daughter with Spina Bifida. She's in a wheelchair."

Orson frowns. "And no husband to help? Shit."

"Yeah. I… uh… gave her a little extra for a private dance."

They all grin. "Out of the goodness of your heart," Kingi says.

"Purely altruistic motives."

They chuckle. Then Linc says, "Must be tough for her, especially at this time of year."

I look back at her. "She told me she's temping at a law firm during the day, so she obviously has to take on several jobs just to make ends meet."

She glances over at the VIP area, and I know she must have seen that I'm not alone. She looks away, her steps faltering for a moment, and it occurs to me that she might feel awkward up on stage, wearing such a skimpy outfit. The dancers who work have chosen their occupation; they know they're going to be objectified, and several have told me they enjoy the attention. They get paid very well for it—better than in most other clubs in London. But Astrid didn't come here to dance, or because she enjoys flaunting her body. I know she's doing it for the money, because the first thing she asked last night, when I asked her if she was going to dance for me again, was, *How much will you pay me?*

I've tried to convince myself that she kissed me because she wanted to. She didn't have to. I didn't promise more money if she did. But maybe I'm kidding myself, and she felt she had to, because I was giving her five thousand pounds for fifteen minutes.

I sigh. I really do have more money than sense.

She lowers to her knees and leans forward on her hands, curving her back as she rocks her pelvis, and a dark desire stirs within me. I can remember the feel of her mouth pressing against mine, and the touch of her tongue on my bottom lip as she requested entry. Her soft moan, and the slide of her hand through my hair that made me rock hard in seconds.

Her long blonde hair coils around her like golden ribbons, and I imagine it slipping through my fingers, silky and smooth. I want her. I want to feel her body against me again. Her soft breasts pressing against my chest. Her mouth opening under mine as she sighs.

I look back at the other men at the table, and discover them all watching her, not speaking as they sip their drinks, the fairy lights sparkling in their eyes. I feel an uncharacteristic surge of jealousy at the thought that they're experiencing the same desire as they observe her, that they want her too.

Without thinking, I slam the drink down on the table and get to my feet. "Astrid!" I bark, my voice carrying across the dance floor, even though the music is loud, the beat thumping through the floor.

She looks at me, astonished. I beckon her to come over. Her eyebrows rise, but she walks down the steps, crosses the floor, and enters the VIP area.

She approaches the nook and pauses in front of the table, shivering a little, hunching her shoulders and wrapping her arms around her.

"Here." I'm not wearing my hoodie tonight, and I slip off my suit jacket and place it around her shoulders.

She looks up at me, surprised, holding the two sides of the front together, and gives a small smile. "Thank you."

Conscious of the others watching with amusement, I glare at them, then say, "Astrid, I wanted to introduce you to some of my friends. This is Kingi, and Orson, and Linc. Guys, this is Astrid."

"Hello," they all say politely, and shake hands with her.

"Will you join us for a drink?" I ask.

"Um, okay." She looks nervous, but lowers herself onto a chair next to where I'm sitting.

"Would you like some of this whisky?" I ask. "Or would you prefer Champagne?"

She gives a short, nervous laugh, then says, "Champagne, please."

I gesture to a waiter for a glass, then sit back down.

"So which of you was the miscreant who introduced Te Ariki to Crystal Palace FC?" she teases.

"That would be me," Linc replies with a grin. "The Eagles are flying high."

"Not really," she says. "They were fighting relegation last time I looked."

I stifle a laugh and have a mouthful of whisky. "These guys own Midnight with me."

"Oh…" She gives them a smile. "So you're the philanthropic crew who hide behind the nightclub."

We exchanged amused glances. "She read my Wikipedia page," I point out.

Kingi chuckles. "You've got no secrets, then."

"None at all," she says cheerfully. "So the Midnight Clubs started in New Zealand, is that right?"

We nod. I gesture at Kingi and Orson. "There was a group of us who used to meet at a club called Huxley's in Auckland, run by a guy called Oliver Huxley. One evening, he told us he was thinking about creating other clubs through the country, but using most of the profits for charity and other good causes. We all thought it was a great idea, and in the end there were over twenty business people who formed the Midnight Trust. Midnight in Auckland was the first resort, but very soon others were popping up all over New Zealand—in the Bay of

Islands, Wellington, Christchurch… There are eight of them now. And then I came here, and we decided to create Midnight in Mayfair."

"Why the name Midnight?" she asks.

"It reflects the fact that most of us work long days," Orson says, "and it's often midnight before we can finally get together and talk about what we really want to do with the money."

"And it makes us sound mysterious and cool," I add, and Astrid gives a delightful girlish giggle that makes my lips curve up.

"It's a great idea," she says softly. "And nice of you all to give something back."

The waiter returns with her Champagne, and she accepts the glass and sips it. Then she swallows hard and says, "Do you want me to dance?"

She thinks I want her to give all of us a personal performance.

"No," I say sharply. "Jesus."

Her eyebrows lift. "I don't mind." But her cheeks flush beneath the fairy lights. She does mind. But I guess she needs the money.

"I just wanted to talk," I state.

"Oh." She glances around the others, who look both bemused and amused at the conversation. She clears her throat. "Okay… so… tell me about yourselves. Are you all married?"

They laugh. "No," Kingi says. "None of us is."

"Aw," she says, "why not? You must have girlfriends waiting at home for you?"

"Nope," Kingi says. "Orson and I are flying back to New Zealand tomorrow for Christmas."

"And you?" she asks Linc. "Hasn't any girl won your heart yet?"

"Not in the UK," I say, and he gives me a wry look.

"So, there's a girl in New Zealand?" she asks.

He sighs and stretches out his legs. "Not really. There was, many moons ago, when I was eighteen. She was the daughter of a deacon."

"Ah," Astrid says, and we grin.

"It wasn't like that," he scolds. "He ran the school I attended."

"For reprobate youths," I say.

"Yep," he agrees cheerfully.

"Tell her how old she was," Orson prompts.

"Yes, okay, she was only fourteen," Linc states sarcastically. "We kinda grew up together, and I was crazy about her. But he caught me giving her our first kiss… and that was that."

Her brows draw together. "Aw."

"Yeah. I left New Zealand and came here, and haven't spoken to her since."

"That's so sad," she says. "Do you think about her much?"

"Every day." His lips twist, and he has a swig of his whisky.

"Seems to me she must be an adult now," Astrid comments. "So it's none of her father's business who she dates, right?"

Linc crunches on a piece of ice, his lips gradually curving up. "She lives thirteen thousand miles away."

"There are these things called planes," Orson says, "don't know if you've heard of them, but they're able to fly you all across the world…"

"It was a lifetime ago." Linc looks away, across the room at the sparkling Christmas tree. "She's probably married with six kids by now."

We exchange glances, all of us aware of how the passing of time changes us.

I look at Astrid and find her studying me with a small smile.

"Don't scowl at me," she says. "It's nice to see you without the hoodie, that's all."

"I wasn't scowling."

"Yes you were. You still are."

"No I'm not. It's the mask. It makes me look cross."

"You scowled before you had the mask," Orson points out.

"Will you shut up?" I gesture at the waiter. "I'm ordering food. Astrid, are you hungry?"

"I skipped dinner," she admits.

"In that case…" I order a couple of platters and some of the focaccia bread the chef makes that's so good.

While the others continue to talk, Astrid leans closer to me and says, "Are you sure you don't want me to dance? I feel like a fraud getting paid for eating and drinking Champagne."

"My club, my rules," I state. "You've been paid, so it's up to me what I ask you to do, right?"

"Right." She looks down at her hands, and I curse myself slightly for my insensitive response. But I can't avoid the fact that I am paying her, and she's only here to make money.

I shove my misgivings to one side though, because Orson starts asking her about her daughter, and Astrid is more than happy to chat about her. I listen as she tells the others about Immi's birth and finding out she had Spina Bifida, about the operations she's had, and what treatment she continues to have now.

It's clear she doesn't have private health care, so she's reliant on the Spina Bifida Association, and the NHS, which does a job but is far from perfect. I remember the wheelchair that got stuck in the cab—it was well worn and clearly secondhand, with a slight rip in the back panel and a wobbly front wheel. She deserves better. But we don't always get what we deserve.

The platters arrive, I sit and eat and drink, not saying much, listening to the guys chatting to Astrid, asking her questions, and her sexy giggle as she responds. Despite obviously not knowing much about business, she asks lots of questions, and the conversation doesn't falter. The three of them are easy to get along with, so I'm not surprised, but it's clear that they're not just being polite. They really seem to like her.

After about an hour, they declare they need to move on—Kingi and Orson have things to do before they fly back to New Zealand tomorrow, and Linc's tired after a week of full-on excavations. I stand and give them all a bearhug, and they shake hands with Astrid, then head through the private exit to their apartments on the top floor.

Astrid remains standing. "I'm going to dance now," she states, letting my jacket slide off her shoulders. I open my mouth to tell her she doesn't have to, but she says, "I want to, it'll make me feel better for accepting the money."

I nod, and she walks across to the stage, climbs the steps, and begins dancing.

I hang the jacket over a chair, sit on the padded-velvet bench, prop my feet up, and watch her. I'm tired, and I should go up to my apartment, but I don't want to leave until she does. So I wait until eleven thirty, when the DJ starts playing slow Christmas songs, and couples begin turning on the dance floor, lit by the fairy lights.

I call her over. She enters the nook, breathing hard, warm now after her dancing, her skin covered with a slight sheen of sweat. "You want me to dance for you?" she asks. When I nod, she pulls the curtain across and comes to stand before me.

Yesterday, she danced in front of me for about fifteen minutes first, but tonight she climbs straight on me, straddling my legs and kneeling on either side of my hips before lowering down onto my thighs.

"I'm glad you took off the hoodie," she murmurs, brushing her hands across my chest and over my shoulders. Her hands are warm on my skin through the cotton, and I can feel her touch more without the jacket between us.

She begins moving slowly to the music, rocking her hips, and she raises her arms and lifts her hair, revealing her slender neck that's just begging to be kissed.

Wondering why I'm torturing myself, I stretch my arms out so I'm not tempted to touch her, and just watch her, fascinated by the way the flickering fairy lights make her eyes glitter and cover her skin in jewels.

Nat King Cole is now singing the *Christmas Song*, and a strange mixture of emotions tumbles around inside me. They say Christmas is a time for children, but it doesn't hold particularly warm memories for me. Hemi and I spent most days alone or with our nanny, playing board games or going outside to throw a rugby ball around, while Dad worked in his office and Mum entertained her friends. We never wanted for toys or whatever food we desired, but Christmas spirit was not something that was abundant in our stockings, and I feel a strange pang of envy at the thought of Astrid going home tonight to her mother and child. They might not have money, and she's obviously suffered a whole range of losses, but they have each other, which is something more priceless than all the gold, frankincense, and myrrh you could buy.

I don't want to think about my childhood, or Hemi, right now. I looked up her name earlier, and Astrid is a Scandinavian name that means 'divinely beautiful'. It's incredibly apt right now, as she tips her head back for a moment, still moving on top of me, then looks back at me, the light behind her making her blonde hair glow like a halo.

She keeps her gaze on mine, leans on the back of the bench, then bends her head so her lips brush mine. Holding my breath, I wait for her to kiss me. She pauses though, for about ten seconds, and eventually I sigh. Her lips curve up, and she moves back a fraction, tips her head the other way, then brushes her lips against mine, once, twice, three times. Butterfly kisses. Light, sensual, and erotic.

I let her tease me, trying not to reveal that my blood is thundering around my body, heading for my groin, and that my breaths are coming fast now. I want her, possibly more than I've wanted anything ever.

And eventually, it becomes too much, and I lift a hand to cup the back of her head, pull her toward me, and crush my lips to hers.

She gasps, her mouth opening, and I take the opportunity to plunge my tongue into her mouth, kissing her deeply as I wrap my other arm around her waist and pull her close against me. For a moment she stills, and I wondered whether I've scared her—customers aren't supposed to touch the dancers, after all. But eventually she loops her arms around my neck and relaxes against me, returning the kiss passionately, and we kiss for a long time, while the music and the fairy lights and the Champagne work their Christmas magic and make my heart lift for the first time in over a year.

Eventually, though, the huge clock on the back wall strikes midnight, making everyone in the club cheer. Astrid lifts her head to look at me, pressing her lips together, and murmurs, "I should go."

Her words sober me up like a glass of cold water thrown over my head. She couldn't have made it clearer. Her time's up. She's just here with me, kissing me, because I paid her. She knows it's a generous amount, and she's conscientious enough that she feels she should give me my money's worth.

"Of course." I stand abruptly, lower her down and set her a foot away from me, take out my phone, and pay her. "Thank you," I say stiffly, willing my erection to go down.

"It was nice to meet your friends," she says softly. "Te Ariki… I'm so sorry about Hemi."

Her comment takes me by surprise. The guys didn't talk about him while she was there, so she must have read about the accident on the Internet.

"It's the anniversary on Saturday," she says, "isn't it? Christmas Eve?"

I give a short nod.

"What do you have planned?" she asks. "You shouldn't be alone."

"I have work to do," I reply. "Don't worry about me."

She walks across to the curtain and pulls it back. Then she glances over her shoulder. "I do," she says simply. Then she leaves the VIP area, and I catch a glimpse of her crossing the floor before she disappears through the doors.

I pick up my jacket and pull it on, then sigh as I realize it smells of her.

Chapter Five

Astrid

The next night, Te Ariki is alone when I arrive at the stage. He doesn't acknowledge my presence, but I can see him watching me as I climb the steps and begin my routine.

The previous evenings, he's sometimes worked on his laptop while I'm dancing, or occasionally spoken on the phone. Tonight, though, he just sits and watches me all evening, sipping his whisky. As eleven thirty approaches, I wonder whether he's going to call me over, and sure enough, as I finish my twenty minutes and make my way down the steps, he beckons to me.

Heart racing, I cross the dance floor, enter the VIP area, and go over to the nook.

"Hello," I say.

"Hey." He's sitting back, his arms outstretched along the back of the bench. He's wearing his suit jacket tonight, but not the hoodie. I'm getting used to the mask now, and my heart skips a beat as his dark-brown eyes survey me steadily.

"You want me to dance for you?" I ask.

He nods. Yesterday, I decided there was little point in beating around the bush and climbed right on top of him, and he didn't complain, so I do the same tonight, settling down on his thighs and resting on the bench behind him while I start to move.

He watches me, his face expressionless, and my pulse betrays my nervousness as I lean in to kiss him. Something feels different tonight. I wonder whether he's cross with me for mentioning his brother yesterday, and for saying that he shouldn't be alone. He's obviously a very private guy, and the fact that he sits here every evening on his own means he doesn't want anyone interfering in his life.

SERENITY WOODS

Or maybe he's just hurting badly, and he doesn't have anyone else to turn to. He broke up with his girlfriend, he's lost his brother, and it doesn't look as if he's close to his parents. He has his friends, but guys don't usually talk to one another about their feelings.

The thought that he might be in pain, physically and emotionally, gets me right in the heart. I slide a hand to cup the right side of his face and brush my thumb against his cheek, look into his eyes for a moment, then kiss him, not teasing him tonight, but trying to tell him instead that I'm sorry for what he's been through, and that if I can make him feel better, even in such a small way, I'm happy to do it.

He sighs, opening his mouth to my tongue, and kisses me back. Eventually he brings his arms around me, and I move closer to him, and we make out for a long, long time. This evening, though, he keeps the pace slow, and I get the feeling he's distracted for some reason.

Finally, as it nears midnight, I lift my head and look him in the eyes. "Are you okay?" I ask.

He gives a short laugh. "Yeah."

"Only you seem…"

"I have something to ask you," he says.

I move back six inches so I can look at him properly. "Oh?"

He stretches out his arms along the back of the bench and lifts his chin, looking me coolly in the eyes. "I want to make you an offer."

I swallow hard. "An offer?"

"Tomorrow night, after you've danced… I'd like you to come back to my apartment and spend the night with me."

My jaw drops as my heart floats up inside me like the bubbles in the Champagne.

"And I'll pay you one million pounds," he adds.

My heart stops dead, somewhere in my throat, and I stare at him.

He's not asking me back to his room as a date. He's going to pay me to have sex with him. Which means he thinks of me as a… oh my God. I can't even bring myself to form the word in my head.

We stare at each other for about twenty seconds, while my mind and heart race. I'm both incredibly insulted and strangely flattered at the same time, and I can't decide which emotion is more important. But more than that is the thought that, for one night, he'll give me a million pounds.

It's an awful lot of money.

"Why?" I say, baffled.

He frowns. "What do you mean?"

"Why me? I'm nothing special."

His expression turns wry, and he just tips his head to the side as if to say, *Women!*

But I honestly don't understand. "I mean it. I'm just... me. I've had the sum total of one partner in my life, and I haven't slept with anyone for two years. I'm out of practice, and I was hardly an expert to begin with."

"I don't want an expert," he says.

"But..." I don't know how to express my confusion.

"There are two caveats," he states.

"Caveats?"

"Conditions."

"I know what it means. What are they?"

"I'll give you one million pounds," he says. "But I will blindfold you. And you have to agree to be restrained."

My eyes widen. "Restrained?"

"I'll tie your hands."

My heart bangs as my chest rises and falls rapidly. He sits calmly, though, waiting for my reaction.

"Why?" I ask eventually.

"I don't want you to see me or touch me." His voice is flat, unemotional.

We're quiet for a while. The fairy lights continue to twinkle, and the DJ is playing some twee Christmas song, but all the festive magic I've been feeling has rapidly fled the building.

He wants to blindfold me, tie me up, and have sex with me. And for that he'll pay me a million pounds. I honestly don't know what to say.

I've been fooling myself. I thought I was beginning to understand the man beneath the mask, but I realize I don't know this guy at all. I'm so incredibly stupid. It's all my own fault. I've been offering myself on a platter to him every night, dancing up on stage with my tits almost out, humping the pole suggestively—why wouldn't he assume I'm happy to sleep with him for money?

I've liked kissing him, because I'm touch starved, and I'm lonely, and I've enjoyed the attention. But I'm so naïve. I'm just Astrid Bergman, a single mum with a disabled child, without two pennies to rub together, and he knows this and thinks I'm desperate enough to agree to have sex with him for money.

And the terrible thing is that I'm tempted.

Suddenly feeling awkward sitting on him, I climb off. I stand in front of him, shivering a little now I've cooled down, wrapping my arms around my waist. "Why a million pounds?"

"What do you mean?"

"You know I have no money. The five thousand you pay me every night is a fortune to me. Why not say ten thousand for the night, or even fifty thousand? Why a million? It's…" I don't know how to express my confusion. "It's a ridiculous amount."

"I want you," he says, with a slight shrug. "I wanted to make it impossible for you to say no."

Again, I feel both insulted and flattered. He wants me. But he thinks he has to pay me to get me.

If, tonight, while he'd been kissing me, he'd asked me to go back to his room with him, would I have gone? I'm not sure, but I'd have been tempted. I like sex, and this guy is charismatic and sexy, despite also being extremely intimidating.

So why does he think he has to pay me? Does he think I wouldn't be interested because of his scars? The article said he hasn't dated since the accident. I know he broke up with his girlfriend after it happened. Was it because she reacted badly when she saw his injuries? It doesn't justify him offering to pay me, but it would explain a lot.

His intense gaze is fixed on me now, his eyes half-lidded. He's thinking about having sex with me. About touching me, being inside me. He wants to blindfold me. Tie me down. Oh dear God. He could do anything he wanted to me once I was restrained, and nobody would be able to stop him.

"I don't know," I say desperately. "I need to think about it."

"Of course. You have a whole day." He tilts his head to the side. "Just remember, a million pounds. And as many orgasms as I can give you." For the first time, his lips curve up.

My face burns. "Jesus."

He notices and gives a short laugh. "Did you think I was only interested in my own pleasure?" His eyes gleam.

I can't reply—I've temporarily lost the power of speech. He's right; I assumed he'd take what he wanted from me and that would be it.

"Orgasms p-plural?" I manage to stutter. Jake was generous in bed and always made me come, but I only ever climaxed once per session.

"Plural," Te Ariki confirms. His gaze turns sultry. "I bet you taste amazing."

I inhale sharply, my eyes widening at the thought of this guy going down on me. While I'm blindfolded. And restrained.

Oh. My. God.

"Think about it," he says, amused. "You can let me know tomorrow night."

I nod. "Goodnight."

"Goodnight, angel."

I walk from the VIP area as fast as I can, and I don't look back.

*

The next day, Friday the twenty-third of December, I call Cora during my lunch break while I walk through Postman's Park. Snow flutters around me, and I turn up the collar of my coat and stuff my free hand in my pocket to ward off the cold.

"Hey you," she says. Cora is the Financial Director at the Spina Bifida Association, which was where I met her six years ago when Immi was born. Coincidentally, she's also from New Zealand.

"You at home?" I ask.

"Yeah," she says. "Just taken some sausage rolls out of the oven. Darren's just eaten one and burnt his lip on it. Serves him right."

I chuckle. Her husband is gorgeous and adores her. They're trying to get pregnant, and I'm hoping the New Year will bring them some good news.

"You still working?" she adds.

"Last day," I confirm. I hesitate. Then I say, "Cora... I need to ask your advice about something."

"Sure. Fire away."

"You know I've been working at Midnight in Mayfair..."

"Yeah..." she says. "How's the Wounded Warrior?"

"That's the reason I'm calling. I've danced for him every night this week, and last night... well..." I swallow hard. "He made me an offer."

"Oh?"

I close my eyes. "He wants me to go back to his room with him tonight."

"Oooh!" She laughs. "You lucky thing!"

"That's not all of it." The words tumble out in a rush, like marbles spilling from an open jar. "He says he'll give me a million pounds. But I have to let him blindfold me and tie me up."

She's silent for a moment. I chew my bottom lip as I imagine the look on her face. Eventually she says, "Sorry, what?"

"I know."

"A million pounds?"

"I know."

"Jesus, Astrid!"

"I know!"

"What did you say?"

"I said I needed to think about it. He's giving me until tonight." Tears prick my eyes. "I don't know what to do."

"Aw, sweetheart… God, what a decision to have to make."

"I feel awful," I admit. "My stomach's in a knot. It's such an incredible amount of money."

"It is."

"I'd be mad to turn it down. Wouldn't I?"

She hesitates again. "That's a decision only you can make, honey."

"I can't." I press my fingers against my lips. "I can't make up my mind. It's so much money. And it makes me angry that he knows it. He said he wants me, and he wanted to make it impossible for me to say no."

"That's quite romantic, in a perverted kind of way."

"Yeah, that's him all over, romantic and perverted. It's just… it would make such a difference to me and my family."

"Astrid…" she says softly, "I know things are tough for you, but you mustn't think that this is the only way out. If you need money, you know I'd give it to you in a flash…"

"I know," I say stiffly.

"Or lend it to you, if you'd rather."

"I don't want to owe anyone anything."

"I understand. I just don't want you to think you have to do this because you have no option."

But the thing is, I don't have an option. Not really. And he knew that would be the case. It's an insane amount of money.

"I just hate the thought of what it will make me," I whisper.

She thinks about it for a moment. "Do you think pole dancers are prostitutes?"

"No, of course not."

"What about those who give lap dances?"

"No."

"So why not just see it as an extension of that? It's entertainment, right? Providing a service?"

I scratch my nose. "I guess."

"Astrid," she says gently, "I think the more important thing here is… do you like him?"

"Well, I did before he offered me money to sleep with him."

"I know it looks bad. But do you think he's a good man?"

I think about the fact that he and his friends created the Midnight Clubs across the world mainly to raise money for charity. I think about how his friends laughed and joked with him, and about everything he's been through. "Yes, I do," I conclude. "And I think he only offered to pay me because he didn't think I'd sleep with him if he didn't. Wikipedia says he hasn't been with anyone since his accident."

"So it's not like you'd be going with an awful guy that you hate just for money, right?"

"No, no."

"Would you have gone with him if he hadn't offered you money?"

I pause, thinking about the way he slid his hand to the back of my head and held me there while he kissed me. "Probably."

"Then honey, what's the issue, really? Are you worried about what people would think? If so, fuck them all. It's nobody else's business. Not mine, not your mum's, no one's."

"Ah, but therein lies the problem. I need to ask Mum to look after Immi all night. And she's going to ask why." I told her eventually that I was dancing at the club, which she thought was most amusing, but she agreed it would have been ridiculous to turn down five hundred pounds a night.

I didn't tell her about the five thousand per night for a lap dance.

"You could tell her you're going to an office party or something," Cora suggests.

"All night?"

"Good point."

I press a hand to my forehead. "Oh, Cora... what the hell am I doing? Why am I actually considering this? He wants to blindfold me and tie me down."

"Is he super kinky, do you think?"

"He said he doesn't want me to see or touch him."

"Aw..."

"I know. But... he could do anything he wanted to me once I was restrained."

She's quiet for a moment. Then she says, "So wishes do come true at Christmas."

"Cora!"

"I'm just saying. You said he was sexy."

I poke a stone with my shoe. "He also said he'd also give me multiple orgasms."

"Multiple?"

"That's what he said."

"Oh my God, you should bite his hand off, then."

That makes me laugh. "It's not as simple as that."

"Of course it isn't. But you said he's a good man. He's sexy. He kisses like a god. He thinks he has to pay you because you won't sleep with him otherwise. And he's afraid of what you'll say if you see or touch his scars. He doesn't sound like someone you need to be frightened of. He just sounds like a wounded guy in desperate need of some love and attention. And I can absolutely see why he might want to pay you a million pounds for that."

I swallow down a lump in my throat. "Thank you."

"All right. You'll let me know how it goes?"

"Of course. I'll call you tomorrow."

"Love you."

"Love you, too." I end the call.

It's given me a lot to think about, but it's not all over yet. I could lie to Mum. I could tell her the club has asked me to work late, or make up some other excuse. But we're close, and she'll know I'm lying to her, and that'll hurt her feelings.

If I don't lie to her, though, and I tell her truth... I know what she's going to say. It's what I'd say if my own daughter was in this situation. The last thing I'd want was for Immi to feel she had to sell her body for money. But equally, Mum knows how hard it's been for me. She has no money either, and barely gets by on the pension she receives after Dad died and the little she can earn cleaning. She gives me what she can, but she knows it's not enough. Is she really going to tell me to turn down a million pounds?

I call her, my heart in my mouth.

"Hello, love," she answers.

"Hey Mum. Look, can you talk? Is Immi around?" She's looking after Immi while she's not at school.

"I can go into the kitchen, hold on." I hear a door closing. "There you go," she says. "What's the matter?"

"Nothing… I just wanted to ask you a favor. Would you be able to look after Immi all night if I asked you to?"

"Yes, of course. Why, what are you up to?"

I chicken out at the last minute. "I've been asked to work at the club."

"Doing what?"

I bite my bottom lip. "It's open all night for Christmas parties. And they're paying really well."

"Ooh, how much?"

I sink onto one of the park benches. It's cold on my butt, but my legs will no longer hold me up.

I can't lie to her. I'm useless at it. And I don't want to.

"A million pounds," I say.

She's quiet for a long time. Then eventually she says, "Sorry, what?"

"You heard right."

"A million pounds?" she confirms. "For dancing?"

"No." And then it all comes spilling out. I tell her everything— about dancing for Te Ariki, and what he's like, and how I met his friends, and how much I like him, even though he terrifies me, and then finally what happened last night, and the offer he made.

The only bit I leave out is about him blindfolding me and tying me up.

When I'm done, we're both quiet for a while. I check the time—I need to get back to the law firm, but I don't want to go until I've finished this conversation.

I know she's going to be disappointed in me. And that hurts more than anything.

I wait for her to berate me. To yell at me. Maybe even to cry.

"Do you like him?" she says.

I press my fingers to my lips and nod, then remember that she can't see me. "Yes," I say, and it comes out as a squeak. "I like him a lot. He's wounded, Mum, physically and emotionally. It's the anniversary of his accident tomorrow, when his brother died, and I don't want him to be alone."

"And I'm guessing he likes you, if he's prepared to pay a million pounds for one night with you? Not that I'm saying you're not worth it." I can hear the smile in her voice.

A tear runs down my cheek, and I wipe it away. "He doesn't think I'll be interested in him if he doesn't pay me. And he said he wants me, and he wanted to make it impossible for me to say no."

"How lovely to be wanted," she says. "Sweetheart, go for it. A million pounds! You'd be a fool not to, right?"

I cover my face, embarrassed and ashamed that I agree with her, and upset that she's being so graceful about her daughter prostituting herself. "I'm so sorry."

"What about? You'll be able to buy Immi that fashion wheel she saw! And Barbies galore! And a new wheelchair, and private treatment for her." Mum's voice turns fierce. "You do it, my girl. For Immi. And for yourself. You both deserve something good in your life."

I nod and squeak, "Thank you."

"All right. I'll see you after work. Don't you worry about a thing."

I end the call, slide my phone into my pocket, and put my face in my cold hands.

Am I really considering doing this? Giving myself to this man for money? This week, I will earn twenty-seven thousand five hundred pounds just for dancing. It's relatively honest work, and it's more money than I ever thought I'd have. Do I really need more? Or am I just being greedy?

But it's one million pounds.

I lower my hands and look up, snowflakes brushing my wet cheeks. Of course the money is why I'm doing it. For me, for Mum, and for Immi.

I'm not doing it because I want Te Ariki. Because I want to feel his mouth on mine again. His hands and his mouth on my body. Because I want to feel him inside me.

I bet you taste amazing.

Oh holy shit. What am I letting myself in for?

Chapter Six

Te Ariki

Astrid appears on stage at seven on the dot.

I inhale with surprise as I watch her climb the steps. A big part of me was convinced she wouldn't turn up tonight. I know she was terrified at the thought of accepting my proposal. But I guess the draw of a million pounds was too much for her to resist.

Of course it was. That was why I offered it. It had to be a large enough sum to ensure she'd say yes.

I feel an odd mixture of exultant and disappointed. Exultant because she came, and although it doesn't guarantee her agreement, there's a good chance she's expecting to sleep with me tonight.

And disappointed because... why? Am I really going to criticize her when I made it impossible for her to refuse? Or look down on her for having sex for money when she's clearly desperate? How cruel would that make me?

And I realize then that I'm not disappointed in her. I'm disappointed in myself.

I should give her the million pounds and tell her she can keep it. That she doesn't have to sleep with me in order to earn it. I'm the one forcing her to make an impossible decision. I can only imagine what Linc, Kingi, and Orson would say if they knew what I've done. Philanthropic businessman, my arse. There's nothing altruistic about forcing a single mom with a disabled daughter to abandon her principles for the sake of money.

I'm despicable, and the worst thing is that I have no intention of changing my mind.

I slide down the bench a little, glowering as I watch her begin to dance. Tonight she's wearing a gold-sequined crop top and shorts that, with her blonde hair, only amplifies her angelic appearance.

I wonder how angelic she is in bed.

Usually I work throughout the evening, reading reports or organizing spreadsheets, but just like yesterday, tonight I can't think about anything else except Astrid. I watch her dance for twenty minutes then leave the stage for a break. Instead of disappearing toward the doors, however, she crosses the room and approaches the VIP area.

Rob, the bouncer, knows her by now and chats to her as he lets her in, and she passes the other nooks until she arrives at mine. She stands in front of me, still breathing heavily from her workout.

I let my gaze slide down her, following the curve of her breasts, the dip of her waist, the flare of her hips, and the length of her legs, all the way to her bare feet. Tonight, she's painted her toenails scarlet. God help me.

I lift my gaze back to hers. "Good evening."

"Hello." She doesn't smile. Her expression is vaguely hostile. "I thought I should tell you that I…" She swallows. "I accept your offer." Her spine is stiff, and she twists her hands in front of her. She's angry and nervous.

"Sit down," I tell her.

She remains standing.

"Astrid, sit. Please."

She lowers onto the chair, her spine straight, her hands clutched tightly in her lap.

"You're sure?" I ask.

She nods.

"You look terrified," I say.

She gives me a look that says, *Well, duh.*

I sigh. "Astrid, I've never taken a woman against her will, and I don't expect to start now."

She studies her hands for a moment. "I'll be okay," she says eventually. "I won't resist."

"Jesus, that's not what I meant."

"Glaring at me isn't going to help the situation."

"I'm not glaring at you. It's the mask."

She rolls her eyes. "That's a convenient excuse for being grumpy." She looks almost sulky. "It's Christmas, for God's sake."

"Bah humbug." That makes her lips curve up, and I smile in response. "That's better," I say softly.

We study each other quietly for a moment. She's still breathing fast, but her spine isn't quite as stiff.

"You're sure about this?" she asks. "You haven't changed your mind?"

I chuckle. "No."

"You're crazy, you know that, right?"

"Certifiable."

She nibbles her bottom lip. "If you're disappointed, will you ask for your money back?"

That makes me laugh properly. "I won't be disappointed."

"I'm very inexperienced."

"You have a child. Clearly you're not that inexperienced."

"That doesn't mean I'm skilled in bed. I don't know any... you know... fancy techniques."

"I'm not asking you to swing from the chandelier."

Her eyes widen. "You have a chandelier in your bedroom?"

"No, it's an expression... will you relax before you strain something? You don't have to do anything. I'm happy to do all the work."

She stares at me. I smirk. Gradually, her face reddens beneath the flickering fairy lights.

"A million pounds and multiple orgasms," I tell her. "Doesn't that sound like a fun evening?"

She doesn't reply, but she does give a small smile.

"You're all right to stay the night?" I ask.

"My mum's looking after Immi."

That surprises me. I assumed she'd ask a friend. "What did you tell her you were doing?"

"I told the truth. I'm terrible at lying."

My eyebrows shoot up. "What did she say?"

She looks away for a moment. "She asked me if I liked you."

I stare at her. Then eventually I ask, "What did you say?"

Her gaze comes back to mine. "I said I like you a lot. And I don't want you to be alone."

She means because of the anniversary of the accident tomorrow. I'm so surprised, I can't think what to say.

Eventually, I add, "So she didn't tell you that you shouldn't come tonight?"

Her expression turns mischievous. "I didn't mention the promise you made about multiple orgasms."

That makes me laugh. "You know what I meant."

"She said, 'I'm guessing he likes you, if he's prepared to pay a million pounds for one night with you.'"

"I do like you."

A frown flickers on her brow. "I don't understand why. I'm not looking for compliments, by the way. I'm genuinely puzzled."

"Because you're beautiful. Inside and out. I saw the way you helped Katie when she fell down the stairs. I wanted you from that moment."

Her eyes meet mine again. I hold her gaze, knowing she must be able to read my desire in my eyes.

She moistens her lips with the tip of her tongue. "Well, I should leave I guess…"

"Stay." I gesture to the waiter and ask for a glass of Champagne. "It might help you relax," I tell her wryly as he goes off to get it.

"I'm not sure it's a good idea to drink right now," she admits. "I'm so full of adrenaline." She looks at my whisky glass. "I saw the bottle. Glenfiddich, right? My dad used to drink that."

Probably not this one, I think, but I just say, "Used to?"

"He died while I was pregnant." She gestures at the glass. "Can I try some?"

I push the glass over to her. "You've had a lot of loss in your life."

She picks up the glass and sniffs it. "Takes one to know one." She sips it, coughs, then says, "Ooh, that's strong."

"It's the smoothest whisky I've ever had."

She coughs again. "I can feel it burning all the way down."

I chuckle and take the glass back. "Here's your Champagne."

She takes it from the waiter and has a mouthful. "That's much nicer."

I smile. "Are you developing a taste for it?"

"I don't think so," she scoffs. "Although I suppose with a million pounds in the bank, I could have a bottle every night." She giggles.

It's such a delightful sound that it makes me grin.

She sips the Champagne again, then puts the glass on the table as she glances at the clock on the wall. "I'd better get back to work."

I don't object, and I watch her as she walks across to the stage, climbs the steps, and begins to dance.

Despite the fact that she looks less professional than a lot of the club's dancers, she draws a lot of attention. I glance around the room, seeing many of the customers, guys and girls, watching her. I wonder whether it's because she's curvier and less athletic, or if it's the fact that she's barefoot. There's something incredibly sexy about her. And she's coming back to my room with me tonight.

My pulse races. One night with Astrid. It's the best Christmas present I could have asked for.

*

Astrid

I'm expecting the evening to follow the same pattern as it has before—me dancing on stage until about eleven thirty, at which point Te Ariki will probably call me to his lair, as I've started to think about the nook. I'm anticipating that I'll give him a lap dance for a while, and following that, around midnight, he'll ask me up to his room.

But tonight is different; each time after I dance he asks me to join him, where we sip Champagne while we sit and talk.

He asks me questions about my life, about Immi, and my friends and family, about where I live and what jobs I do. Later, around ten p.m., he asks me about Jake, and I wonder whether he's been thinking about him while I've been dancing. I tell him a little about my husband, feeling guilty as I describe him as quiet and unambitious, and quickly add that he was kind and gentle, too.

"He was very different from you," I say, then realize how that sounds. "Oh, I mean… I'm not saying you're not kind and gentle…"

He doesn't reply, his eyes glittering in the fairy lights, and my mouth goes dry. Just because he gives money to charity doesn't mean he's kind and gentle in bed.

"He had depression," I continue. "I knew when I married him, but I didn't realize how bad it was. I spent a long time blaming myself for not doing more to help him. But the truth is that you never know what's going on inside another person."

"That's true."

I clear my throat. "What about you? Tell me about Hemi." I say it before I think better of it, then remember he didn't like me looking him up on Wikipedia. "Well, you don't have to…"

"He was two years younger than me," he says. "He was smart and funny, as well as kind and gentle." He gives me a rueful smile. "You would have liked him."

"His death must have been very hard for your family."

He looks at his whisky. "Yeah."

"Are you close to your parents?"

He swirls the whisky over the ice in his glass. Then he says, "No."

I wait for him to say more, and when he doesn't, I reply, "So you won't be seeing them for Christmas?"

"No."

"Where will you be spending Christmas Day?"

He finishes off his drink and places the glass on the table. Then he looks at me and holds out his hand. "Come here."

Surprised, I put down my glass of Champagne, stand, and walk over to him. He gestures for me to climb on his lap, and I do, kneeling on the bench on either side of his hips.

"You want me to dance for you?" I murmur.

His gaze drops to my mouth. "No."

"You didn't answer my question."

"I know." He lifts a hand to the back of my head and pulls me down to kiss him.

I think he's doing it to keep me quiet, or partly at least, but I can't complain because he's kissing the living daylights out of me, holding me tightly to him, and I don't even have room to breathe. I give a small moan as he delves his tongue into my mouth, and he just growls in response and deepens the kiss.

He moves his head back and looks at me, and his eyes are dark, the pupils huge. "Will you come upstairs with me?"

"It's only ten thirty."

"I want you now," he says.

A wave of panic washes over me, but I keep a lid on it and just nod. "Okay." It'll probably be better to get it over with, I tell myself.

I lift off him. He picks up his phone and types something, presses a few buttons, waits, gets a text message, and puts in the code. Then he turns it around to show me. It's a banking app, and on the display is a transaction—the transfer of one million pounds from Te Ariki Thompson to Astrid Bergman.

Holy fuck.

He pockets his phone and hesitates. "It's your choice now," he says. "If you want to walk away, you can."

I stare at him. "You mean I don't have to sleep with you?"

He shakes his head. "The money's yours either way."

My jaw drops. He's giving me the opportunity to keep my... honor, I guess, for want of a better word. He's saying he'll give me one million pounds... for nothing. Why? Because I have a disabled daughter? Because my husband died? And my father died? Because he feels pity for me? My face flames. For some reason, I have no idea why, that feels even worse than selling my body. I refuse to take out loans or take money from my friends or family, and I'm certainly not going to accept charity from a stranger. I have more pride than that.

No, my choices are: give the money back, or take it and go through with it.

His eyes gleam, and I realize then that he knew this would happen. He knew I wouldn't walk away with the money. I hate him a little for that. But it's not his fault that I can't take the cash and run; it's mine. They're my skewed principles. And I have to live with them.

He looks a little amused. I think he's actually quite enjoying my roiling emotions, and that makes me cross.

"I'm not afraid of you," I say irritably. Made braver by the Champagne, I add, "You think because of your scars that you're super scary, but I think your attitude is all for show."

He doesn't reply.

My stomach flips at the sudden thought that I'm baiting the guy who's about to tie me up and have sex with me. "I just need to get my bag," I say hurriedly. "Then you can take me upstairs."

His lips curve up, but he doesn't stop me climbing off him.

I leave the nook and walk fast across the room and down the stairs to the changing rooms, pick up my bag, then return upstairs. I don't talk to anyone on the way. If someone were to question what I'm doing, I know I'd turn and run in the opposite direction as fast as I could.

Without another word, he takes my hand and leads me over to the back wall of the nook. He opens the hidden door, and it swings inwards to reveal a small corridor with a lift. A private entrance? Very swish. He presses the button, and we wait a few seconds in silence for the doors to open.

We go inside, he presses the button for the top floor, and the lift begins to rise.

I open my mouth to comment on the fact that he obviously has the penthouse, but before I can say a word, he strides across the carriage, takes my face in his hands, and crushes his lips to mine.

I gasp, and he takes the opportunity as my lips part to slide his tongue into my mouth as he pushes me up against the wall.

"Mmph…" Whatever I'm trying to say comes out muffled.

He lifts his head and looks down at me. "Are you going to complain every time I kiss you?"

"It wasn't a complaint. You took me by surprise, that's all."

"You've gone pale."

"I think I'm hyperventilating."

"You want to put your head between your knees?"

I give a short, slightly hysterical laugh and try to calm my breathing. "No…"

He strokes my cheeks with his thumbs, looking down at me. He's so tall, and so much bigger than me. There's a soft light in the lift, but it's brighter than it was in the nook, and I get my first good look at his face. The mask he wears is obviously tailor made for him, and it fits snugly, covering most of his forehead, half his nose, and curving around his mouth, which appears to be untouched by the scars.

I wonder how far down he was burned—it's tough to tell as I've only ever seen him in a wing-tipped shirt. His hands look okay.

His eyes are a beautiful chocolate brown with gold flecks. He's clean shaven, and his jaw looks smooth, as if he had a shower and shave just before meeting me.

He's not the only one who spent time preparing himself; this evening, after giving Immi her dinner, I had a bath, shaved my legs, slathered them in cream, and made sure the rest of me was hairless and smooth. It's been a long time since I've got myself ready for a man. And it's stranger when we've never even been on a date.

"You're so beautiful," he murmurs. "Just like your name."

"I'm not bad looking," I say doubtfully, "but I'm not worth paying a million pounds for."

He moves closer, pushing me up against the wall again, and my heart pounds.

"I already know you're going to be worth every penny." His voice is husky with desire.

He lowers his head to kiss me again, but the doors ping and open, and I duck under his arm and out of the lift. Chuckling, he takes my hand and leads me along the corridor. The pile of the carpet here feels about six inches deep, soft on my bare feet, which make no sound as we walk. There are only four doors in the corridor, two to the left and two to the right, so presumably there are four penthouse apartments. Do they belong to Linc, Kingi, and Orson? I wonder how often they stay here, and how much time Kingi and Orson spend in England.

I don't get a chance to ask Te Ariki, though, because he's already opening the last door on the right, and as I walk in all thoughts flee my mind. The apartment is huge. I'd read that it looks out over Green Park, but it feels as if I can see the whole of London, the city lights sparkling in the darkness through the falling snow.

The carpet is a deep pile again and cream; as we walk across it, all I can think is how difficult it would be to get a glass of red wine or blue crayon out of it. The suite is cream too, and leather; the cushions are burgundy, and the furniture is all chrome and glass. What I'm sure is very expensive artwork hangs on the walls—abstract paintings that look as if Immi has drawn them. I don't mean to be harsh when I say that. I love my little girl with all my heart, but I could never call her an artist.

It's a beautiful apartment, spacious and elegant, and it doesn't look as if he spends any time here at all.

"It's a lovely place," I murmur as he leads me through to the huge kitchen.

"It's okay," he says.

The kitchen is spotless and shining, with every mod con you could ever need, and again, it doesn't look as if he ever sets foot in it. I'm guessing Chef Bernard cooks all his meals and he has them sent up. He goes over to the fridge and extracts a bottle of Champagne, then gestures at the cupboard. "Can you get two glasses?"

I bring two tall glasses out while he pops the cork, and he pours the golden bubbles into them. He hands me one, and I sip it, conscious of his hot gaze on me. I'm tempted to down the glass in one, desperately in need of some Dutch courage, but equally I don't want to pass out in the bedroom. Whatever he says, he might decide he wants his money back if I don't show a little enthusiasm.

To my surprise, he tucks the bottle of Champagne under one arm, then holds his other hand out. I slide my tiny one into his big bear paw, feeling his warm fingers close around mine. I give him a shy glance as he leads me out of the kitchen and then across the living room to a corridor.

Partway along, he stops and says, "Just a sec," and goes into a room on the left. It also overlooks Green Park, but this time it isn't the view that makes my eyes widen. The room is a large study, with bookshelves lining the inner wall. A large oak desk and a big leather office chair are at one end of the room, the table covered with heaps of folders, papers, and books. At the other end, an exquisite black leather sofa that looks soft and comfortable faces the biggest widescreen TV I've ever seen. A PlayStation sits beside it, next to a rack of both games and Blu-Ray movies. The coffee table in front of the sofa is covered in more books and papers. The whole place smells of his cologne, and the color scheme is burgundy and midnight-blue: strong, masculine colors. This is where he spends his time.

While he crosses to the desk, takes out his phone, and leaves it there, I go over to the coffee table and pick up a couple of the books he's been reading. Two of them are about property investment: *The Intelligent Investor* and *Rethink Property Investing*. There's also a book that's a history of rugby union, and another one called *Black Gold*, which is about the All Blacks—the New Zealand national rugby team.

I hold the former up as he approaches. "*A Game for Hooligans*? Is that you?"

"It used to be." He holds out his hand again. "Come on."

I put the book down, realizing with embarrassment that he probably can't play much sport now. I take his hand again and follow him out and along the hallway.

"I'm sorry," I murmur. "I didn't think."

"Don't worry about it." He turns left, and I find myself in a bedroom.

It's large, square, and once again faces Green Park. Like the study, it bears the imprint of his presence. There's another comfortable sofa here, facing the windows, and more books on the coffee table in front of it. A door in one wall stands ajar, revealing a walk-in wardrobe and a rack filled with suits and shirts. A large chest of drawers sits against the inner wall. Just along from it is a real log fire, the flames crackling happily in the grate providing the only light in the room—someone's been in here to light it. A thick rug rests in front of it, made for lying on and making out by the fire.

And in the middle of the room is the bed. Oh... it's a four poster, and it's fucking enormous. I've heard that an emperor-size bed exists, but I've never seen one. It must be at least seven feet square. The posts are wooden and carved, and it has a fancy headboard. The bedding is all black. It looks like the kind of bed a billionaire would have.

It's sumptuous and decadent, but the only thing I can think is that I'm shortly going to be tied to those four posts, and my knees start to shake.

Snow falls like a white curtain outside the big windows, giving me the sensation of being cut off from the world. I'm alone with Te Ariki. I doubt anyone could hear me scream, and even if they did, I'm sure they wouldn't come running. It's just me and him. He's going to blindfold me and restrain me, and then he'll be able to do whatever he wants to me for the rest of the night.

Oh. My. God.

Chapter Seven

Te Ariki

I take off my shoes, remove my jacket, and hang it up in the walk-in wardrobe.

When I come back out, Astrid is still standing in the middle of the room, shoulders hunched, clutching her Champagne glass. Her eyes are the size of dinner plates, and they widen even more as I come out.

"Penny for them?" I say as I go over to the chest of drawers.

"No." I raise an eyebrow, and she clears her throat. "I mean… I'm not thinking of anything."

I give her a wry look as I open the top drawer. "I sincerely doubt that."

"It's just… in that shirt… you look so big… and I was wondering whether you're going to…" Her voice trails off as I extract a long black scarf. "Fit," she finishes, her voice little more than a squeak.

I hide a laugh. "Will you relax? You're going to enjoy yourself, I promise." I walk over to her and stand before her. The thought of sliding inside her, a fraction of an inch at a time, of her being tight around me, makes me as hard as a rock.

She looks around her. The pulse in her neck is beating rapidly. I lift a hand and cup her cheek. "Relax," I say gently. "You're not in danger here. You're free to leave at any time."

"Even when I'm tied up?" She trembles.

"Astrid, if you want to go, you just have to say. And I want you to tell me if there's anything you don't want me to do."

"I don't want to be tied up."

"Except that. That's non-negotiable."

She chews her bottom lip, then lifts her chin and looks me in the eyes. "I don't want to do anal."

"I wasn't planning on that anyway, but noted."

"And I want you to use a condom."

"Of course."

"I don't want you to hurt me." Her eyes glisten.

I frown at that. "Honey, I don't find pain sexy. I promise you, if at any point you feel anything less than pleasure, you only have to say, and I'll stop immediately. Do you understand?"

She nods, apparently slightly mollified. She takes a deep breath. Then she looks around. "Can I use the bathroom?"

I gesture at the *en suite*. "Take as long as you need."

She picks up her bag, walks into the bathroom, and closes the door, taking her Champagne with her.

I purse my lips, pour myself another glass, and take it over to the window. My heart is racing too. It's been over a year since I made love to a woman, and although I haven't forgotten how to do it, exactly, I am nervous.

Unbidden, the image of Sara May's horrified face flashes into my mind, and I cover my eyes with my hand and massage my temples, wishing I could erase the memory. It's okay, I tell myself. Astrid won't be able to see me or touch me. To her, I'll be the old Te Ariki, the man many women called handsome, who was known as a skilled lover. She'll never see the real me, and I'll never have to see that look of revulsion on her face.

There's a click as the bathroom door opens, and I turn to look at her. My eyes widen. She's changed out of her dance outfit, and now she's wearing a beautiful cream satin chemise or nightie, I'm not sure which it is. It has spaghetti straps, and it reaches to mid-thigh. Two long slits on either side go all the way up to her hip, revealing her pale legs. The sides and the material around her breasts is edged with lace. She's brushed her long blonde hair, and it hangs almost to her waist. She truly looks like an angel.

"You look surprised," she says. She's carrying her glass, and she finishes off the Champagne as she approaches.

"I didn't expect you to change."

She glances down at herself. "I wore this on my wedding night." She looks up at me then, and her face reddens. "I'm sorry, I shouldn't have said that. It's not very romantic to talk about previous partners."

I move closer to her, take her glass, and put it with mine on the dresser. Then I return to her. "You look absolutely stunning," I murmur.

She moistens her lips with the tip of her tongue. "Thank you."

I lower my lips to hers and kiss her, just a brush of my mouth against hers. The lower half of my face wasn't damaged by the fire, so I'm able to kiss without worry, but I'm always conscious of the mask, and I'm eager to be rid of it. So I move back and lift the scarf I'm still holding in my left hand.

"Are you ready?" I ask.

She looks at the scarf and nods. Her breasts rise and fall rapidly as her breathing quickens, but she doesn't move.

I walk around her until I'm standing behind her. I fold the black silk scarf over until it makes a band, then lower it in front of her face, and she closes her eyes. I cover them, then tie it at the back.

"How does that feel?" I ask, checking that she can't see.

She nods. "Okay."

I return to the back and tie it in a bow, making sure it's secure. Then I circle her again and stand in front of her.

I take my mask off, and drop it onto the chest of drawers. I return to her and take her face in my hands.

Then I lower my lips to hers and kiss her properly.

Aaahhh… it's bliss to be free of the mask, and not to feel the pressure of it against my skin. It's specially made and supposed to help minimize scarring, but I still hate the thing.

Relieved of it, and without the fear of Astrid's reaction, I feel almost like the man I used to be. Joy floods me, and I murmur with pleasure as I kiss her, enjoying the feel of her mouth beneath mine. There's not a single angle on this girl's body; she's all curves and softness. As I continue to kiss her, she sighs, her breath whispering across my lips, and I feel a little of her tension dissipate.

"Have you taken the mask off?" she asks.

"Yes."

"I thought so. You kiss differently without it." She trembles a little.

"Don't be afraid of me, Astrid." I kiss her mouth, her nose, her cheeks, over the silk scarf covering her eyes, and around to her ear. I kiss the lobe, then suck it into my mouth, and she inhales. "I don't want to take anything from you," I say softly, and tug the lobe lightly with my teeth. "I want you to give yourself to me freely."

"I'm here," she says. "My very presence is consent, isn't it?"

"That's not enough."

"It's all I've got."

"For the moment." I kiss back down her jaw to her mouth again, and brush my lips against hers. "I'm going to make you beg." I kiss one corner of her mouth. "Beg me to kiss you." I kiss the other side. "Beg me to taste you." I kiss the center. "Beg me to let you come." I run my tongue along her bottom lip. "Beg me to slide inside you."

"Oh my God," she whispers.

I tilt my head, changing the angle, and as her lips part, I sweep my tongue into her mouth. I'm hungry for her, and this time I don't hide my desire, kissing her deeply. My hand slides to the back of her head, holding her there, and I let the beast inside me devour her, kissing her until she groans, until her hands tighten to fists on my chest and her knees buckle. I catch her before she falls, though, and sweep her up into my arms.

She clutches hold of my shirt as I carry her, and I lower her onto the bed. She shivers, and for a moment I think it's either fear or desire, but as I slide my arm from under her legs I feel her skin. Of course, she's been barefoot all evening. She was probably okay while she was dancing, but now she's feeling the cold.

"Do you want me to put another log on the fire?" I ask.

"No, it's nice and warm in here. It's just my legs and feet."

"Well, we can't have that. Get under the covers."

"Okay." She pushes the duvet down and slides beneath it, then runs a hand over the top. "Is this Egyptian cotton?"

"I didn't bring you here to talk about fabric."

She pokes her tongue out at me.

I get another scarf out of the chest of drawers and climb onto the mattress. Then I move on top of her, kneeling, my hands on either side of her head, and look down at her. "Are you being sassy to me?"

She sucks her bottom lip and shakes her head.

Lips curving up, I say, "Arms above your head."

For a moment, she doesn't move. Is she going to refuse? I'm not going to tie her up without her permission. I stay where I am, looking down at her. Eventually, slowly, she lifts her arms above her head.

"Hands together," I instruct. She moves them together, crossing her wrists.

I had the headboard imported from New Zealand. It's made from Kauri wood, carved into Māori patterns—korus, hei matau, or stylized fish hooks, and pikorua, or twists. The center of the twists form holes right through the headboard.

I pass the scarf through one of the holes and back through the one next to it. Then I tie the ends around her wrists, binding them together, not too tightly, but tight enough so she can't wriggle out.

When I'm done, I sit back and look down at her. She trembles slightly, but again I'm not sure if it's from nerves or because she's cold.

Slowly, I begin to undress.

Astrid swallows hard. Then, surprising me, she says, "Do you have a tattoo?"

I stop in the process of unbuttoning my shirt, alarmed. "Can you see me?"

"No. But I thought I caught a glimpse of it through your white shirt before you blindfolded me. It looked like a full sleeve."

I continue unbuttoning. "It is."

"What's it of?"

"Māori patterns, like the ones on the headboard." I take off the shirt and toss it away, then look at my arm. "My brother had a similar one. He had his done first, and said I should get one to match. He said it illustrates our genealogy and our love for Aotearoa." It's the Māori name for New Zealand.

"That's nice," she says.

I open and close my hand, flexing the arm muscle. "I asked why I would want to display a connection to my family that doesn't exist, and I pointed out that we were living in the UK. But he said that our hearts belong there, and in the same way we'll always be a part of our parents and our family."

"That's a lovely sentiment."

I give a harsh laugh. "The fire destroyed about two-thirds of it. A not-so-subtle hint from God."

"What do you mean?"

"Hemi was the one who rang our parents every week, who stayed in touch, and who asked for their advice. Now, I don't speak to them at all. I'm sure God was trying to tell me that my link to my parents has been severed, and I don't deserve to wear that link to my family or my country." Jesus, why am I telling her all this? The whisky has loosened my tongue.

"Te Ariki," she says, "it was an accident."

I clench my jaw. "I was flying the plane, remember?"

"Even so. It wasn't your fault."

Her forgiveness brings unexpected tears to my eyes, and I climb off her, hating the suddenness of the emotion. "I don't want to talk about it," I say bluntly as I undo my trousers. She doesn't reply.

I take the trousers off and toss them aside, flick off my socks, then remove my underwear. Finally, I retrieve a packet of condoms from the bedside table and leave them on the top before climbing onto the bed and sliding under the duvet.

I move up close to her and look down at her.

"I'm sorry," she whispers. "I didn't mean to upset you."

I study her lips, which are pale pink and look soft and kissable. Without saying anything else, I lower my head and kiss her. She jumps a little, as if she wasn't expecting me to do that, but she stays still.

Moving even closer to her, wanting to make sure she's warm, I hook a leg over hers. Then I kiss her again. I press my lips across hers, then kiss up her cheeks, across her nose, over the blindfold to her forehead, and nuzzle her hair. "You smell nice," I mumble, inhaling the scent of her shampoo. "And your hair is so shiny." I lift a strand of it in my fingers, and it slips through them like a silk ribbon.

Placing a finger on her forehead, I draw it down her nose, over her mouth and chin, down her throat, and over her breastbone. As I continue between her breasts, her nipples pucker and protrude through the satin fabric of her nightie. I cup one breast and brush the nipple with my thumb, and she sighs, which turns into a light moan.

"You might look like an angel," I say huskily, "but you were made for sin." I pinch her nipple lightly, and she gasps and tries to draw up her knees, but she's unable to do so because I'm half lying on her.

I kiss her, this time sliding my tongue into her mouth, and she moans again. I'd wondered whether she might be too scared to do anything but lie there, but she kisses me back, her tongue thrusting against mine. I'm not sure whether it's all an act, though, whether she feels she needs to put on a performance to give me my money's worth. There's only one way to tell, and I'm determined to find out.

I kiss her for a long time, exploring her body with my one hand beneath the covers. I stroke her breasts and down over the silky nightie, trail my fingers over her stomach, then brush across her hips and down the outside of her thigh.

"Your legs aren't as cold as they were," I murmur.

"It's getting warm under here," she whispers. She's drawn up one knee, and I push it gently. She resists for a moment, and I lift my head and look at her.

"Astrid," I scold. "Do as you're told."

She swallows, then lets her knee fall to the side, parting her legs.

I rest my hand on her knee, then brush my fingers up the inside of her thigh. Very, very slowly.

She's breathing fast, and her nipples are standing out like buttons through the satin fabric. I watch her moisten her lips with the tip of her tongue as I brush back down her thigh. Her skin is incredibly soft.

"Do you like that?" I ask, lowering my head so I can touch my lips to hers. "Do you like me touching you?"

"Yes," she whispers.

"Can you tell how much you turn me on?" My erection is pressing against her other hip.

"Yes," she says. "It's hard to miss it."

I chuckle, stroking back up her thigh, then brush my fingers across her mound. Finally, I slide them between her legs. She's silky smooth, hairless, and already swollen.

"Aaahhh…" I sigh and then groan as I slide my fingers down into her and find her wet and slippery. "Astrid… already?"

"You're shocked? You've been torturing me for ages."

Even so, I'm surprised, and now so turned on I can feel my heart banging on my ribs. I draw some moisture up over her clit and circle the pad of my finger lightly over it, and her teeth tug on her bottom lip.

I kiss her cheek as I arouse her. "It would be so easy to slide inside you right now," I murmur. "To thrust us both to an orgasm. But where's the fun in that?"

"It sounds like a lot of fun to me." Her voice comes out breathless.

"I don't want to rush this. I want you aching for me, Astrid."

She groans. "I'm already there."

"You're nowhere near where I want you." I kiss down her throat, touching my tongue to the hollow at the bottom, then continue over her collarbone and down to her breasts. Cupping one and pushing it up so the nipple pokes through the fabric, I cover the tip with my mouth and gently suck. The wet satin clings to her skin, and she shudders, then moans as I tease the nipple with my teeth.

I swap to the other one, sucking until the satin there is wet and her nipple has puckered, then return to the first, teasing and sucking and flicking them with the tip of my tongue. Her hands flex in her restraints, and she writhes beneath me, arching her back and pushing her breasts toward me, so I know I'm turning her on.

Eventually, I lift up, hold the duvet so it doesn't slide off her, and move beneath it, on top of her. I look down at her, bend my head, and kiss around to her ear, then whisper into it, "I'm going to taste you now."

"Oh God…"

"He's not coming to help you, my little fallen angel." I kiss back down her body, and this time continue all the way down, shifting until I settle between her thighs.

It's semi-dark beneath the covers, and warm. Glad she's no longer cold, I press my lips to her right thigh and kiss up the soft skin, then do the same to her left. I kiss across her mound, and then finally I press a hand on either side of her and expose her to my gaze.

She says something unintelligible, it might have been, "Oh God," again, and tenses beneath me.

So I wait, and instead blow gently across her sensitive skin. She groans.

"Slowly, Astrid," I scold. I brush a finger down, just touching her, and she trembles.

"Te Ariki," she whispers, and I sigh, loving the way she says my name.

I stroke her all the way down, then turn my hand palm up and tease her entrance with a finger. After a while, I add another finger, inserting them just a half inch, coating the tips with her moisture. She moans, and so I continue to do it, setting up a steady rhythm, until she begins to move her hips to match it.

Then I stop and remove my fingers, and she sighs.

I insert my fingers in my mouth and suck them. "Mmm. I knew you'd taste sweet," I tell her.

"Jesus. I knew you'd be a pervert."

That makes me laugh. "It's perverted to like the taste of your woman?" It's only as the words leave my mouth that I realize I said, "your woman" and not "a woman". It implies that I think of her as mine. I think about how I felt a sweep of jealousy when the other guys were watching her dance, and realize that maybe I do think of her as mine. She works for me, though. She's a part of the club, and the club is mine. That's all I meant.

I lower my head and slowly lick all the way up her, from her entrance to her clit.

She jerks and cries out, and I place a hand on her thigh. "Steady," I tease.

"You have to warn me when you're going to do that," she says, panting.

"I really don't." I do it again, and she jerks, then groans as I cover her clit with my mouth and suck gently.

"You're trying to kill me," she mutters. "You're trying to sex me to death."

I stifle a laugh and just continue licking her.

Aaahhh... the sweet taste of her, the way she's so swollen and ready for me... it's bliss. I press two fingers on either side of the hood covering her clit and expose the tiny button, circle the tip of my tongue over it, then suck it again. At the same time, I slide two fingers back into her, this time deep inside her, and she groans and tightens around them, tilting her pelvis up to encourage me to suck her.

She's not far from coming, I think, and I feel a surge of exultation at the thought that she's not faking this. A man can never truly tell, but I've been with enough women to feel confident that I know how to turn them on, and Astrid is nowhere near difficult to arouse.

Briefly, I wish her hands were free so she could slide one into my hair; I'd love to feel her nails scrape against my scalp, and her fingers tighten as she comes. But that's not possible, and I push the thought away, lifting my head and removing my fingers.

"Oh..." she says, sounding disappointed. "Oh God, I was so close..."

"Aw, Astrid, were you?"

She huffs a sigh. "You're doing it on purpose. I hate being edged."

I stroke down, keeping my touch light. "Why?"

"Because... ohhh... it makes me ache..."

"But that's a good thing. The deeper the ache, the more intense the orgasm."

She doesn't reply, and so I lower my head and lick all the way up her before covering her clit with my mouth and sucking.

"Fuck," she says loudly.

That makes me laugh, and I lift my head again and kiss her mound. "Language."

"Fuck you."

"Ah… the real Astrid is making an appearance." I tease her with my fingers.

"Oh God…" She gives a long, drawn-out groan. "Te Ariki…"

"What?" I touch the tip of my tongue to her clit and flick it.

"Please…"

"Please what?" I thrust my fingers agonizingly slowly into her, take them out and lick her moisture off, then do it again.

"Argh… ohhh… please…"

"You have to be more specific." I continue to slide my fingers in and out of her, and intersperse my sentences with brushes of my tongue.

"You want me to beg," she says breathlessly.

"I do." I suck her clit briefly, then stop.

"Oh God…" She trembles. "Please…"

"Please what, angel?" I remove my fingers and blow across her skin.

"Ohhh… please… let me come…"

"Mmm." With smug satisfaction, I kiss her thigh. "Good girl. Now hold on. This is going to be a tad overwhelming."

I slide my fingers back into her and stroke them firmly, then cover her clit with my mouth and suck.

She trembles again, her breathing turning ragged and uneven, and then gasps and clenches around my fingers as she comes. Her clit pulses on my tongue, and I continue to suck it, sharing in her ecstasy and loving every minute of it as she shudders and cries out with pleasure. As I'd hoped, it goes on for a long time, and when the pulses eventually stop, her chest heaves and she says, "Oh my God, oh my God…"

I remove my fingers and give her one last kiss, then lift up and press my lips to her tummy, her breasts, her throat, and finally her mouth before settling down on top of her.

"I knew you'd taste amazing," I tell her, then kiss her deeply, delving my tongue into her mouth and sinking my hand into her silky hair. Oh, she's beautiful, this girl, and I can't wait to take her and make her mine.

Chapter Eight

Astrid

Te Ariki is heavy on top of me, pressing me into the mattress, but I discover that I don't mind one bit. My body is still humming from my orgasm, as if I'm a tuning fork he's struck. The root of his erection is nestled between my legs, and when he rocks his hips, he grinds right against my sensitive clit, which makes me groan.

It's bizarre, making love blindfolded and restrained. I've never done it before. Jake was very religious, and although he enjoyed making love, of course, he once admitted that his mother had told him as a boy that sex was purely for making babies and that doing it for any other purpose was a sin, and I'm sure that guilt was partly why he wasn't particularly adventurous in bed. Being with Te Ariki is a very new experience. Not being able to see does heighten your other senses, and I guess it is erotic to think your partner can do anything he wants and you're not able to stop him. But part of sex for me is touching the guy and observing his pleasure.

"Te Ariki," I murmur when he eventually leaves my lips to kiss my throat.

"Hmm?"

"Will you take off my blindfold?"

Immediately, he stiffens and lifts his head to look at me. "I told you there were two conditions," he growls.

"I know. I'm asking you to change your mind."

"Why?"

"Because I want to look in your eyes while you make love to me."

He's silent then, and even though I can't see his face, I'm convinced he's astonished.

Eventually, though, he says, "No."

I frown with disappointment. "They're just scars," I say softly. "They're nothing to be ashamed of. You're not going to shock me."

"You say that." His voice is flat and unemotional. "That's not been my experience."

"Your ex," I say softly. "Sara May. Is she the reason? Did she react badly when she first saw you after the accident?"

He doesn't reply, so I know I'm right. We can only judge based on our own experiences, and he's convinced that all women are going to react the same way.

We're silent for a moment. He's still on top of me, but he's breathing heavily, and I can feel the resentment and irritation flowing from him. He's not going to agree to remove the blindfold no matter what I say. And he won't untie me either. Unless…

"Will you untie my hands if I agree not to touch your scars?" I ask.

I wait, heart thumping, but he doesn't say anything. He hasn't refused either, though.

"You can trust me," I say. "I want to touch you, not your scars."

When he still doesn't reply, I try again. "Wouldn't you like to be touched? Wouldn't you like me to kiss your body?"

"Yes," he says, his voice hoarse.

My heart flares. "You can show me where I can touch you, if you like."

He pauses for so long that I'm sure he's going to refuse. Eventually he lifts up, and I inhale as I think he's about to demand that I leave.

But he just sits back, and then he leans over me and unties the scarf binding my wrists. I can't help but smile.

"Don't be smug," he says.

I giggle. Then I feel him lift my right hand. "Show me," I whisper.

He lifts my hand to his face, and I extend my first two fingers. I already know where he must be burned because of the shape of the mask, but he shows me where I'm allowed to touch. He brushes my fingers from the right side of his forehead, down the right side of his nose, and across his lips. He continues down the middle of his neck, then draws them across his collarbone, almost to his left shoulder. There he stops and changes direction, brushing my fingers beneath his arm to his elbow, then along his forearm. So his left shoulder and upper arm where the tattoo is are obviously burned.

He links our fingers for a moment, and for some reason my heart leaps because it feels like such an intimate gesture, which is bizarre.

Then he takes my hand again and returns it beneath his arm. He flattens my hand so it's resting on his chest and draws it down, so my fingers just touch the side of his ribs, then lets it rest on his waist and brings it right across his body. No scars on the front, then.

Taking my other hand, he brushes it all the way down from his neck, over his shoulder, and around his back, sliding it under his arm and letting me touch his spine and a little past it before bringing it back. He sighs as I brush over his hips, apparently enjoying the feel of my fingers on his skin.

"Okay," I say softly. "My turn."

I place both hands on his chest and widen them, exploring the areas of his body that he's marked as clear. Lightly, I stroke up to his neck, then use the fingers of my left hand to touch his face and lips, and he turns his head to kiss them. I slide them into his hair and glide them over his scalp, then bring them down and over his shoulder, stroking all the way down his arm, my right hand joining in as I touch his forearms and hands.

Next I rest my right hand on his chest while I slide my left around his back, and I trace the muscles there. Finally, I rest my nails at the top and score lightly down the right side of his spine.

He shudders, grabs my hands in his, and pins them both above my head.

"Was that nice?" I say silkily.

"Yes." His voice is little more than a growl, and he bends his head and crushes his lips to mine.

I'm no longer afraid of this man. He's damaged, physically and emotionally, and his ex's reaction to his scars obviously burned him far deeper than the fire. He's been curled up in his lair licking his wounds, too frightened to venture out. But in here, with me wearing the blindfold, he's able to be the man he was, and I discover that I like him very much.

I only have one night with him, though, and I'm determined to make the most of it.

I wrap my legs around his waist, tilting my hips up so I arouse myself on his erection, and he groans against my mouth, kissing me more deeply, plunging his tongue inside. When he eventually leaves my lips and kisses down my throat, I say, "Can I kiss you, too?"

He stops, surprised, I think, then says doubtfully, "If you want."

I pat the bed next to me, and he shifts off me, turning to lie on his back. I lift up, feeling to make sure I know where to touch him, then lean over him and look down. "I know you're used to being in control," I say. "But for once you need to lie still, okay?"

He huffs a sigh, but he doesn't protest. So I lean over him and press my lips to his, then begin kissing the rest of him.

I kiss the right side of his face, up over his closed eyelid and eyebrow, then his temple and around to his ear, touching my tongue to the lobe and giving it a quick suck. Then I continue down his neck, pressing my lips to the hollow of his throat, and carry on down his sternum, then across to his right nipple, which I circle with my tongue.

Next I kiss his right shoulder, lifting his arm so I can kiss each finger and his palm, and then brush my lips up his forearm and his biceps before returning to his chest. I do the same with his left hand, kissing each finger, then kiss up his forearm to his inner elbow.

I feel him inhale as I reach there, so I know I must be close to the scars, and I lower his arm carefully to the bed before I get to them.

Lifting up, I kiss down his ribs to his belly, which is flat and taut, and murmur my approval as I shift on the bed.

Finally, I circle my fingers around his erection. He groans, lifting his arms, and I think he might be covering his face with his hands as I lower my head and close my mouth over the tip.

A bead of moisture has formed on the end, and I remove it with my tongue, swallow, then lick my lips.

"Fuck," he says.

"Slowly," I scold, echoing his admonishment, and he huffs a laugh, then sighs loudly as I cover the tip with my mouth and slide my lips down the shaft. Ooh, he's not a tiny man, and it makes my jaw ache as I take him as deep as I can while brushing my tongue around the head.

"Astrid," he says, but I ignore him and continue to suck, only stopping when he grasps me by the upper arms and hauls me up his body. "For fuck's sake, girl," he says. "I only have so much willpower."

I lick my lips. "You taste nice."

"Christ." He flips me onto my back, making me gasp. The mattress dips as he leans across, then I hear the sound of a foil wrapper being torn. My heart picks up speed as he sits back, and I know he's rolling the condom on.

After he's done, he grasps my nightie by the hem, draws it up my body and over my head, then tosses it aside. Gently, he pushes up my knees, and then I feel him move the tip of his erection down to my entrance. He presses against it, parting me, and enters me a little. Then he stops, and he leans forward, resting a hand on either side of me.

"Relax," he instructs.

I try. I really do. But it's been so long, and I'm nervous about how it's going to feel, and I know I'm tense when he finally pushes forward. Ooh… he feels big. I stretch to accommodate him, and gasp at the exquisite sensation.

He only enters me a little, and then he withdraws. While my chest heaves, he does it again, this time going in a bit more before moving back. I realize he's coating himself with my moisture, trying to make it easier.

The bed dips as he bends, and his lips touch mine. "You're incredibly tight." he says, his voice husky.

"Sorry."

"It wasn't a complaint. But I don't want to hurt you. Try to relax."

I inhale, then blow out the breath, doing my best to release the tension that's built up inside me.

"Good girl," he says, and he pushes his hips forward again. "Stop me if it hurts."

"Mmm… that feels good," I say, sucking my bottom lip as he continues to slide inside me. So he carries on, and gradually—a half inch at a time—he enters me, until he's all the way in, and our bodies are flush.

"Fuck." His voice is a low growl.

"Mmm." I clench inside, tightening around him. "Oh God, that's so good."

"Jesus. Are you trying to make me pass out?"

I giggle, then realize that I'm not scared anymore. He's so gentle and considerate. I know he's not going to hurt me, and my tension finally dissipates.

Then, slowly, he begins to move.

I'd forgotten how fantastic sex can be, and what it feels like to have a man inside me. I haven't thought about it much at all since Jake died; I've been so busy looking after Immi, and just surviving takes all your energy. But I've always loved sex, and all my old feelings come flooding back; the deep, dark, joyful desire that rises through you at the feeling that you're joined with a man in such an intimate way; the wicked sensation that you shouldn't really be enjoying it quite so much as you are; the intense urge to fuck the guy's brains out until he erupts and spills inside you.

He kisses me for ages while he moves inside me, and *aaahhh…* it's heavenly. He's starting to find his rhythm, and I moan as he pushes his hips forward, burying himself in me so deeply that I'm sure he's trying to spear me to the bed, before he starts to move with purpose, thrusting hard.

He catches my right hand in his left and pins it above my head, and I know he's doing it so I don't touch his left side, but I don't complain, happy to use my other hand to touch him. He crushes his lips to mine, and I explore his back and hip and butt as he thrusts, digging my nails into the plump muscle there and enjoying the movement of it beneath my hand as he moves.

The Champagne has had an effect, and it's hot in here now, and I'm so turned on that I'm beginning to lose the plot a little. Te Ariki won't stop kissing me, and I can barely breathe as he thrusts his tongue into my mouth. Just as I think I might be able to come soon, though, he lifts up, and to my surprise he withdraws from me.

"Aw," I say, and I'm about to complain when he takes my arm and pulls it across me.

"On your front," he instructs.

Heart racing, I turn onto my tummy, tugging a pillow down to clutch a hold of.

"Lift up," he says, patting my butt, and I push up and feel him tuck another pillow beneath me, lifting my hips.

He nudges my legs apart, pushes up my left knee, and positions the tip of his erection against my entrance. Slowly, he enters me, sliding inside me, and I bury my face in the pillow, groaning out loud at the sensation of him filling me up.

"Oh my God, that feels so good," I whisper, widening my legs to give him better access.

"You feel fantastic," he confirms. "So fucking hot and wet."

"Language," I tell him as he begins to move.

In response, he smacks my butt, making me jump, but he just laughs and lowers down to kiss my neck. My lips curve up. I love him like this. Playful and oh, so sexy…

I bite my bottom lip as he sets up a fast pace, thrusting hard, his hips meeting my butt with a sharp smack. I bury my face in the pillow, holding on for dear life while he rides me, hardly able to catch my breath. Holy shit… I'm not going to be able to walk tomorrow…

"I'm going to come," I mumble as everything starts to tighten, expecting him to stop, but he doesn't; he rides me through it, and I squeal out loud and clamp around him, gasping with every pulse.

"I told you there would be multiple orgasms," he murmurs in my ear as he withdraws. He helps me up, then to my surprise, bends and picks me up, wrapping my legs around his waist.

I squeal and grab hold of him, and my fingers brush his shoulder briefly, touching the puckered skin there before I remember and move them to his chest. For a second I expect him to yell at me, but to my surprise he doesn't say anything as he walks across the floor. I wonder if he's going to put me on the chest of drawers, but then I feel cool air to my back, and…

"Ow!" I yell as he presses me up against the glass. "Ooh, that's cold!"

He gives a mischievous chuckle, and then I feel him pressing into me, and he's inside me again, lowering me down so I'm impaled on him a second time.

"Ah," he says, his mouth close to my ear, "I wish you could see this. It's snowing behind you. It looks amazing."

I know better than to ask him to take off the blindfold and just sigh, my fingers tightening on his left shoulder, while my right hand presses against his chest.

"You're so beautiful," he murmurs in my ear. "I feel like I'm fucking an angel."

"That's not very godly of you."

"I don't feel very holy right now."

"I'm not surprised." I groan as he thrusts, and flatten my right hand against the glass.

He keeps me there for a while, holding me up with one hand while he teases a nipple with the other, the steady rhythm of him inside me drawing me to the edge once more.

Eventually I groan and say, "Oh God, I think I'm going to come again…"

"Not yet." He slows his pace. "Hang in there, girl."

"Ah, please…"

He withdraws, lifts me off the glass, turns, and carries me back across the floor. Then I feel him dip, and heat blooms on my left side, and I realize he's lowering me onto my back in front of the fire. The rug is soft and lush beneath me, and the warmth of the fire makes me feel as if I'm glowing.

He kisses my face. "Are you comfortable?"

"Yes…"

"You look amazing in the firelight. You're so beautiful, Astrid."

Tears prick my eyes beneath the blindfold. "Thank you. I wish… I wish I could see you."

"I know." He kisses my mouth, slides inside me, and starts to move slowly.

I sigh and give myself over to him, to his luscious kisses and his long, slow thrusts, feeling my body stir once again as he teases me toward the edge of pleasure. He's heavy on top of me, and deep inside. My senses are overwhelmed with the feel and taste of him, the scent of his cologne, and the touch of him beneath my fingers.

"Yes," he says, and for the first time I sense that he's losing control. His hips move faster, more urgently, and his hand tightens in my hair, while his kisses become more intense.

I'd like to come with him, but my own pleasure is building, and I can't hang on any longer. "Oh God," I say, and he kisses my mouth, my cheeks, and over my blindfold as he says, "Yeah, baby, come for me."

"Ahhh…" I suck my bottom lip, concentrating on the gradual tightening of my internal muscles. The orgasm feels as if it's coming from a mile away, and I moan as the pulses begin, washing over me with intense pleasure, and forcing me to clench around him.

He says something, but I don't hear what it is, and he's thrusting hard, and then he stiffens and exclaims, and I feel his body harden beneath my fingers as he comes. His hips jerk, and I know he's feeling that same blissful feeling, and I stroke his back, so glad I could do this for him, and loving every second.

He lowers his forehead to my shoulder, and we lie there as our breathing slows, drifting down to earth along with the snowflakes outside.

Mmm… I'd forgotten how amazing the afterglow of sex is. All those pheromones and hormones swirling around, making me feel happy and extremely content. He sighs, and I stroke his back, liking the feel of his hot skin, and the sensation of him giving tiny thrusts as he enjoys the final few moments of being inside me.

Oh God, it's so hot in front of the fire. I blow out a breath, feeling my skin sticking to his, and sweat sliding down my face beneath the blindfold. I pat Te Ariki's back, but he doesn't move. Jesus, I'm melting... Lifting a hand, I push the blindfold up and off my hair with a groan—

And then I freeze. I did it without thinking. As he lifts his head, it's impossible not to see the damaged skin on the left side of his head and body.

I look into his eyes, inhaling sharply as horror fills me. Not because of his scars, but because I know I've transgressed the unwritten law. I've seen the man behind the mask, and instinctively I know he'll never forgive me for it.

His eyes widen too. For a moment, we freeze, neither of us knowing what to do.

Then he rips out of me and rears back, lifting an arm to cover his face.

"Wait," I say in panic, but he scrambles to his feet. He backs away, bumping into the chest of drawers.

"What the fuck?" he yells. He grabs his mask and tugs it on, then picks up his shirt and yanks it up his arms and over his shoulders. Only when his scars are covered does he turn and snarl, "I *told* you not to remove the blindfold."

I rise hurriedly, my heart pounding. "I'm so sorry, I didn't think..."

"You had to fucking spoil it." He grabs his boxers and pulls them on. "Get your clothes."

My eyes widen. "What?"

"Get dressed. I want you to leave."

I stare at him. "Come on, let me explain..."

His eyes blaze. "Get out."

I stand my ground. "Calm down and talk to me. Your scars... they're not as bad as you think they are."

"Did I ask your opinion?" His bitter tone, so soon after our lovemaking, hurts me to my core. "Get dressed, or I'll call security and have you thrown out, and I don't care if you don't have a stitch on."

Anger flares inside me at the ridiculousness of the situation, but I grab my bag and yank out my underwear, jeans, and sweater, nervous in case he carries out his threat.

"Will you stop!" I snap as I tug on my knickers. "I wasn't shocked at what I saw. It was just that I knew you'd asked me not to, and because I knew you'd overreact. I wonder what made me think that?"

He puts his hands on his hips, chest heaving.

"I wasn't shocked by your scars," I tell him again, quickly doing up my bra and then pulling on my jeans. "Please believe me."

He glares at me. "You broke your promise. How can I trust anything you say? You got your money, now get out."

He thinks I'm saying what he wants to hear because he paid me. My eyes sting as I tug on my sweater. I can't blame him. I took his money. And I did break my vow to keep the blindfold on. Why should he believe me?

Once dressed, I walk up to him and rest a hand on his chest. "Please, don't do this." I look him in the eyes. "I'm not scared of you."

He meets my gaze for a moment. His eyes are full of pain and betrayal, so incredibly hurt that it makes me want to curl up like a poked spider.

Then he picks up his Champagne glass and, before I can say anything else, draws back his arm and throws it at the wall where it smashes, scattering pieces across the carpet.

"Well, you fucking should be," he shouts.

I flinch and cower, shocked and upset by his fury. Trembling, I pick up my bag. Carefully avoiding the glass, I take out my shoes, slip them on, then walk to the door.

I turn and look at him. His hands are clenched into fists, and his eyes are blazing.

"It's not your fault," I say as calmly as I can. "You didn't kill Hemi."

"Get out!" he roars.

As quietly as I can, I slip through the door and let it close behind me.

I run through the apartment and out through the door, then, because I don't know any other way, I return the way I came, going down in the lift and out through the secret door into the club.

As I run across the room, the music thumping loudly in my ears, the clock on the wall strikes midnight, and everyone cheers. The irony doesn't escape me, as I exit the club and go out into the snow.

Chapter Nine

Te Ariki

My door has a buzzer, and when it sounds, I open my eyes and blink in surprise.

"Astrid?" I sit up unsteadily and look at my phone. It's close to one thirty a.m. I stare at the bottle of whisky on my study table. It was a new bottle, but I've been drinking steadily since she left, and a good portion of it has vanished. I must have passed out around twenty minutes ago.

The buzzer sounds again, and I get to my feet. I'm tired, drunk, and angry, and I know I shouldn't see her while I'm in this mood. But the thought that she's returned still fills me with joy.

I scowl. No, I'm not happy, she broke her vow, and I'm furious. I stride through the apartment to the door, and I tear it open, getting ready to vent my frustration and pain on her.

The words catch in my throat when I see not Astrid standing there, but Linc Green.

"What the fuck are you doing here?" I demand.

He frowns and walks past me into the apartment.

"Hey, I asked you a question." I catch his arm and yank him around.

He lets me, and raises an eyebrow. "You want to punch me, bro? Because better me than Astrid."

I glare at him. "I wouldn't hit her."

"Maybe not, but you sure as hell scared the shit out of her."

My glare fades. "You've seen her?"

"She called me and told me what happened."

I stare at him blankly. "How did she know your number?"

"She asked Miranda."

The alcohol is making it hard for me to process his words. "Why did Astrid call you?"

"Because she knows it's the anniversary of the accident today, and that it's going to be tough, and she was worried about you."

"Fuck her," I snarl.

"Yeah, yeah," he says, "blah blah, you're Zeus up on Mount Olympus, and we're all your minions. I'm going to make some coffee."

"I don't want coffee."

"You're going to drink it, and then we're going to talk about what an idiot you are and come up with a way that you can make it up to her." He goes into the kitchen and turns on my coffee machine.

"What if I don't want to make it up to her?" I demand, shoving my hands in the pockets of my track pants.

"Then you're a fucking idiot." He pops a capsule in the top. "She's the best thing that's happened to you in a long time, and you'd be a fool to let her go."

I glower at him. Then, not sure my legs will hold me up, I sink onto a bar stool, lean on the counter, and put my head in my hands.

"She told you what happened?" I mumble.

"She was very worried about upsetting you."

"She saw my scars," I whisper.

"Yeah, she told me."

"She broke her promise."

"Not on purpose—she was hot in front of the fire and took the blindfold off without thinking."

"She told you I blindfolded her?"

He glances at me. "She told me everything."

Ah, shit. She told him that I offered her a million pounds to have sex with me. His look makes me feel an inch high. I've been such an idiot.

"She was terrified of me, Linc," I whisper.

"No, she wasn't. She said your scars weren't half as bad as she expected, and the reason she looked alarmed was because she'd promised not to look, and she knew how angry you were going to be." He takes the cup from the machine and slides it across to me. "She really likes you."

"She only likes the money," I say morosely.

"Oh shut the fuck up," he snaps. "Have you checked your bank account?"

"No."

"Well, do it now."

Blearily, I take out my phone and bring up the banking app. I stare at the list of transactions.

She's rejected the payment I sent her.

"How did she do that?" I ask, stunned.

"There are such things as banks that work twenty-four-seven. I'm guessing it's not every day that someone asks to send back a million pounds."

My jaw drops as I stare at the phone. "She returned the money?"

I rest my elbows on the counter, and put my head in my hands.

He's silent for a while as he waits for the machine, and then I hear him walk around the counter. "Come on, bro," he says, resting a hand on my shoulder. "Let's go and sit in the comfy seats."

I lower my hands, pick up my coffee, and follow him over to the suite. It's snowing heavily, the flakes falling at an angle, caught by the breeze up here at the top of the building. I think about how I pressed Astrid up against the glass, and how beautiful she'd looked with the white curtain behind her.

While he sits in an armchair, I sink onto the sofa and have a big mouthful of coffee. I don't want it—I want whisky—but the hot liquid sears down inside me, and although it doesn't sober me up exactly, the strong, earthy taste is oddly grounding.

Astrid was upset and distressed when she left here, and I sent her out into the cold night without checking that she got home all right.

Staring into the cup, I say, "I've fucked everything up."

Linc sighs. Then he says, "Nah."

"I gave her money to have sex with me. You don't think that was the wrong thing to do?"

"It was totally the wrong thing to do, but she understood why you did it. That your addled brain thought no woman would want you unless you paid them."

"I insulted her."

"Well, yeah, but honestly? I think the worst bit was assuming she'd have the same reaction to your scars as Sara-fucking-May."

I stare moodily at him. "Is this supposed to be cheering me up?"

"No. It's supposed to be making you come to your senses." He leans forward, elbows on his knees, cradling his cup in his hands. "The three of us—Kingi, Orson, and me—we could see how hard you'd taken Hemi's death, and we knew it was pointless to try to convince you that it wasn't your fault. So we agreed we'd give you a year to grieve. Three hundred and sixty-five days to blame yourself and hide in your lair like a wounded animal. And that year's up, my friend."

"Not for another twenty-two hours."

He gives me a wry look. Then he sighs again, and his expression softens. "You've been through hell, man. You lost your brother and your girlfriend, you've suffered horrendous physical wounds, and you've also been vilified by the press, because they're cunts."

I give a short laugh. "You're sounding more and more English with each passing day."

"It's true, though. What the press have done to you—it's disgusting."

"I deserved it."

"No, you didn't."

"Yes," I say calmly. "I did. I've been incredibly arrogant. I thought I was better than everyone else."

"Well, you kind of are."

"No, I'm not. I was rich and good looking, and I thought it meant I was superior. Your analogy of Zeus on Mount Olympus was right—I felt as if I was a god, gazing down on the insignificant mortals who looked like ants to me."

"So that's why you haven't fought back," he says softly. "Because you agree with them."

I just sip my coffee.

"Te Ariki…" He pauses. "Yeah, okay, you were arrogant—it's impossible not to be, when you're rich and you look the way you do."

"Looked."

He leans back, surveying me for a moment. "You know how self-pitying that sounds?"

I don't reply.

A frown flickers on his brow. "Why do you hate yourself so much?"

"I've just told you."

"No, you were the same before I met you. You covered your positive traits in a veneer of disdain, but you were a kind person with a huge heart. You've raised millions for charity." His expression turns incredulous. "Was it all about balancing the scales? Trying to offset all the bad things you felt you did?"

I look away, out at the falling snow.

"In medieval times," Linc says, "Catholics used to buy indulgences in an attempt to reduce the amount of punishment they had to undergo for their sins. That's what you're trying to do with the money from Midnight, isn't it? To attempt to pay for redemption." He looks puzzled. "I don't understand. Why do you think you're such a bad person?"

I look back at him. "Because I was born into money. And I've spent my whole life using it to get what I want."

"And yet it can't buy the things that really matter to you. It can't buy a woman's love. It can't buy your father's respect. And it can't bring Hemi back from the dead."

We study each other for a long time.

My chest heaves with emotion. The whisky, the late hour, the evening with Astrid and our argument, and now Linc's incredibly acute observations, are smashing through my tight self-control, and it's all crumbling down around my ears.

"He's gone," Linc says simply. "And it wasn't your fault, bro. The landing gear seized. Nobody could have landed that plane."

"He wasn't going to come to Scotland with me. I talked him into it."

He snorts. "Nobody could talk Hemi into doing anything he didn't want to do. His death… your accident… it was a fucking shit thing to happen. But it was just one of those things. You can't change it, no matter how much you give to charity, or how much time you spend metaphorically whipping yourself with a flail. And the same goes for your father."

I sink my hand into my hair. "Don't start."

"Bro, I'm not one to talk about perfect son/father relationships. My dad despises me. But one thing I have learned is that I will never, ever be able to change how he feels about me. All I can control are my own reactions and emotions. You can't make your father love or respect you. But you can learn to accept that neither of those things is going to happen, and realize that all that matters is how you feel about yourself."

"Are you charging for this advice?"

"You can be as sarcastic as you like, my friend. I'm just trying to help."

I massage the bridge of my nose. Linc's one of the good guys, and he doesn't deserve my mean spiritedness, especially on Christmas Eve. "I know. I'm sorry."

"So… what are we going to do about Astrid?"

I lower my hand. "I was very angry with her."

"I know."

"She didn't deserve it."

He tips his head to the side. "So what are you going to do about it?"

"What can I do? I've insulted her. Yelled at her. Who would ever forgive behavior like that?"

He finishes off his coffee and puts his cup on the table. "I suppose it depends on how you feel about her. Was she just a one-night stand? Do you just feel guilty because you behaved badly? Or do you feel bad because you might have lost a woman who was honest-to-God an angel in disguise?"

My eyes prick with tears. "Are you trying to make me cry?"

"Jesus, no. If you start bawling, I'm outta here. Look, if she was just a fling, just a girl who took your fancy, that's okay, it happens, and you handled it badly, but it's probably best you move on and let her get over it. But if it was more than that… if you really liked her, and you think there could have been something good there… well, you know what you have to do, right?"

"Say sorry?"

"Yeah, dude! Grovel like you've never groveled before. The whole shebang—on your knees, hands clasped, begging for her forgiveness."

I slide down the sofa, rest my head on the back, and look up at the ceiling. "I can't believe she rejected the payment. Her husband died two years ago, and her father died when her daughter was born. The girl is disabled. Astrid has no money. Not a single penny. She's working two or three jobs just to pay the rent. And she gave back a million pounds."

"Why do you think she did that?"

"Because it made her feel cheap?"

"Well, yeah. But I was going to say because she wanted to show you how she feels about you. She told me that if you had asked her to go to your room tonight, and you hadn't mentioned money, she would still have gone."

I stare at him. "Seriously?"

"Yeah. She likes you, bro." He smiles.

I lift a hand and touch the mask absently. "She really said she wasn't frightened by the scars?"

"Yeah. I think she, more than anyone, understands that who you are inside is as—if not more—important than what you look like on the outside."

I think about her little girl, and the way she lifted her out of the car, hugged her, and kissed her cheek before lowering her into the wheelchair.

"You're not the devil," Linc says. "You're really not that interesting."

I lean forward, elbows on my knees, and rest my mouth on my clenched hands.

"When I arrived at the accident," he says softly, "I could see that Hemi was already dead, and you were badly burned. I knew it was going to be extremely hard for you physically and emotionally. But I pulled you out of the flames anyway, because you're my friend, and because I believe you're one of the good guys. I'm so sorry he died, and I know part of you died in that plane with him. You'll never stop grieving. But it's been a year, and it's time to start living again."

My hands, jaw, and eyes are all clenched tightly, but I'm still unable to stop tears leaking through my lashes.

"Time for me to go," he says. "I'm just down the hallway if you need me." He rises, walks to the door, goes through, and lets it close behind him.

I can't hold it in any longer. The emotion is too strong—it's like being hit by a tsunami. I give a deep gasp that hurts my throat, and then cover my eyes as the tears come. Tears I've held in for a whole year.

The grief pours from me, raw and painful. But like any storm, eventually it dies down, and finally it passes.

I flop back onto the sofa and turn my head to look out at the snow. And I think of Astrid. Her long golden hair. Her delightful giggle. And the way she looked at me, shyly, with desire in her blue eyes.

You know what you have to do, right?

I watch the snow fall, and even though I'm incredibly tired, it takes a long time before my eyes finally close.

Chapter Ten

Astrid

I wake to my daughter's loud squeal, and her yelling, "Mummy! Mummy!"

I leap out of bed, bleary-eyed, before I'm even properly awake. We share a bedroom, because it's only a two-bedroom flat, and I wanted my mother to have the other room because she pays half the rent, plus it's easier for me to help Immi if she needs the bathroom in the night.

"What's the matter?" I demand.

"Look!" Wide eyed, Immi points at the window sill, which is covered in a thick layer of white. "It's been snowing!"

I blow out a long breath, my heart racing, but I'm unable to hide a smile. "Come here, crazy girl." I bend down, and she loops her arms around my neck, and I lift her up. I carry her over to the window, and we look out at the view of the street. It's not as impressive a view as the one from Te Ariki's apartment, but it's not bad. It's an incredibly tiny flat, but it overlooks Camden Lock. The water is still flowing, but the narrowboat moored up on the opposite side is covered with snow, and the pavements are untouched by footprints. It's nearly eight a.m., but I guess the weather and the fact that it's Christmas Eve has kept people inside.

"Oh!"

I turn at the sound of my mother's voice behind me. "Hey," I say with a smile.

"I didn't hear you come in," she says. "Is everything okay?" She comes over and rubs Immi's back.

"It's snowing," Immi says, pointing at the lock, and Mum glances down with a smile.

"Wow, how perfect for Christmas," she says. Then she looks at me. "Are you all right?"

"I'm fine." I turn away. "Come on," I tell Immi, "let's get you dressed, and then I'll make breakfast. I bought some bacon! Would you like an egg and bacon roll?"

Her eyes light up. "Ooh, yes please."

It's cold in the flat; electricity is so expensive, and we've been trying to save money on the heating by wearing thick clothes. But I have twenty-seven thousand five hundred pounds sitting in my bank account. I think this Christmas I can splash out.

"Can you put the fire on in the living room?" I ask Mum.

She gives me a look that says, *This conversation isn't over*, but she goes out. I help Immi pull on her socks and a sweater over her pajamas, then do the same myself before taking her through to the bathroom. Afterwards, we go through to the living room, and I sit her on the sofa and turn on the TV.

Then I start making breakfast. The kitchen is connected to the living room, so when Mum comes over and leans a hip against the counter, I give her a warning look.

"She's watching the TV," she says softly. "So… what happened yesterday? I thought you were going to be there all night."

"I decided not to stay." I turn the stove on and put a little oil in the frying pan.

"Astrid." She touches my shoulder. "What happened?"

I turn the pan to coat the base with the hot oil, and sigh. "He didn't want me to see his scars, and when I looked at them by mistake, he got very angry, so I left. I didn't take the money, Mum. I couldn't."

She gives a long, sad sigh. "That's okay, sweetheart. I understand."

"I know it would have made a huge difference to us, but—"

"It's all right."

"I've still got twenty-seven grand. If we're sensible with it, it should last us a long time."

"Of course. We'll be fine. We've been all right so far, haven't we?"

I nod, although we both know it's not going to get any easier. As Immi grows up, she's going to need more clothes, schoolbooks, and all the other things that kids need as they make their way toward adulthood. Despite her disability, I want her to have as many opportunities as other kids—I don't want it to stop her doing anything she wants to do.

My phone is sitting on the kitchen counter, and it buzzes now, announcing an incoming call. I glance at it and see Cora's name. "Can you watch the eggs?" I ask Mum. "It's Cora."

Mum takes the spatula from my hand, and I pick the phone up and answer it. "Hey you," I say, walking out of the living room and through to the bedroom.

"Hey. How are you doing?"

"I'm okay." I go over to the window and watch the snow still falling thickly.

"Where are you?" she asks.

"I'm at home."

"You didn't stay the night?"

"No." I sigh and tell her what happened as briefly as I can. It's impossible not to get choked up as I describe how angry Te Ariki got when he realized I'd seen his scars, but I take a deep breath and explain that I left the apartment, then returned his money when I got home.

"Ahhh…" she says, "hmm, well maybe that explains it."

"Explains what?"

"Well, the Association office is closed for Christmas, but I'm still checking my emails and the accounts at home. This morning, someone made a huge anonymous donation."

I blink. "How huge?"

"Ten million pounds."

My jaw drops and my eyes widen. "Holy shit!"

"I know. For some reason, you were the first person I thought of. Your guy, he's really rich, right?"

"He's not my guy," I say sadly.

"Are you sure about that?" I can hear the smile in her voice. "Ten million pounds is an awful lot of money."

"It might be his way of saying sorry," I concede, "but that doesn't make him my guy."

"Aw. What are you going to do now?"

I shrug. "What can I do? He wanted one night with me, and he got it. Our transaction is complete."

"I can't believe you gave him back the million pounds."

"I know. I must be fucking crazy."

We both give a short laugh.

"I'm so sorry," she murmurs. "You really liked him, didn't you?"

"Yeah, I did."

"Was he good in bed?"

"Oh my God, you have no idea."

She sighs. "All right. I'll see you later?" She's invited me, Mum, and Immi to join her and her family for the evening.

"Yeah, of course. See you later."

"Love you."

"Love you." I end the call.

I sit on the bed for a moment, fighting against tears. I can still feel Te Ariki—my body holds the memory of him in the ache of my muscles, and I'm sure I can smell his cologne on my skin. I close my eyes, remembering lying on the soft rug in front of the fire, and the feel of him moving inside me while he kissed me. It was such a wonderful evening. I can't believe I ruined it by lifting the stupid blindfold.

But ultimately, even if I hadn't, it wasn't going to lead to love and forever, was it? Maybe one day he'll find someone who he'll allow to get close to him, but that woman was never going to be me.

I press my fingers to my lips and fight against my emotion. Only when I've wrestled it under control do I go back into the kitchen and help Mum finish the bacon and egg rolls as I tell her what Cora's just told me about the anonymous donation.

"Do you think it was him?" she asks as we carry the plates into the living room.

"I'm convinced of it," I say. "I don't know why he did it."

She just smiles. "I think I can guess."

She means because of me, and I suppose she's right. It must have been a kind of apology. It's a lovely gesture, and I'm thrilled for the Association, but it makes me sad that he didn't come and tell me personally. Oh well. I guess that's the last I'll see of him.

We eat the rolls together, watching the morning show with its Christmas music and recipes, and then we shower and dress, and Immi starts getting excited because I've told her we're going to go out and make a snowman.

"I must be mad," I mumble to myself as I carry her down the three flights of stairs because the lift isn't working again.

"Join the club," Mum says, puffing as she carries the wheelchair. "We need to complain to the council. This is ridiculous. There must be some law against making us do this with a disabled girl."

"Not at Christmas," I scold. "The other fifty-one weeks of the year, we can rant and rail at the authorities, but not this week."

"Maybe we can get a lighter wheelchair from the Association, as you're responsible for the big donation."

"We don't know that, Mum, and even if he was, I can't take advantage of it."

She continues to mumble beneath her breath, and I smile as I negotiate the rest of the stairs and then finally emerge into the foyer. Mum opens up the wheelchair, and I lower Immi into it, make sure she's comfortable, and then we head outside into the wintry morning.

"Ooh, it's cold!" Mum shoves her hands deep into the pockets of her coat.

"Come on," I say, pushing Immi forward onto the pavement and along to the small square. The benches and pots with small trees are hidden by the snow, but I park her next to a bench so she can scrape the snow from it, and together we start making a snowman.

Mum helps me roll the snow into a large ball, and we make a smaller one and place it on top of it. By this point our noses are red and our hands are frozen, but Immi's eyes are bright, and the cold is worth her enjoyment.

"We need a carrot for his nose," she says.

"Hmm, maybe we'll have to use a stone," I reply. I scrabble about in the plant pot and extract a large round pebble. "How about this?"

She claps her hands. "Yes! And others for his eyes."

I push smaller black stones in for his eyes, then stand and stare at the snowman's face. Reaching out a finger, I begin drawing a line. I start at his right temple, and draw it around his nose, across his cheek, up the left side of his face, and across the top.

"What's that?" Immi asks.

I lower my hand. "A friend of mine wears a mask like this."

"Why?"

"Because he was burned in a fire, and he doesn't like people looking at his scars."

"That's a shame," she says.

"I think so."

"It's not a great likeness," a voice says from behind me. "I don't think my nose is that big."

I spin around, my jaw dropping. He's wearing jeans and a thick black hoodie with the hood up, but he lowers it now, revealing a red-and-blue-striped Palace scarf wrapped around his neck.

"Oh," Immi says, spotting his mask. "It's your friend!"

I've lost the power of speech, and I can only stare at him as he surveys me calmly, then smiles at Immi.

Mum comes to the rescue. "You must be Te Ariki," she says warmly. "Hello. I'm Hannah."

"Nice to meet you," Te Ariki says, shaking her hand. "And this must be Immi. Pleased to meet you, Immi."

Shyly, she shakes his hand. "We're making a snowman," she says.

"I can see that. With a mask."

"Like yours," she says.

"Yes, like mine."

"Were you only burned on one side of your head?" she asks.

My mouth opens to tell her not to ask questions, but he glances at me, then looks back at her and says, "Yes, that's right. And my left shoulder and arm."

"How did it happen?"

"In a plane crash."

"Did it hurt?"

"Yes, a lot, at the time."

"Does it hurt now?"

"Sometimes. The skin is quite tight, and it can get sore."

"I get sore," she says, "on my back where I had the operation. I have to take medicine for it."

"I'm sorry to hear that."

"Was it you?" I ask, finding my voice at last. "Who made the donation to the Association this morning?"

He glances at me again, but he doesn't reply. I can see from his expression that it was him, though, and I exchange a glance with Mum, whose eyes shine.

"Come on, Immi," she says. "Let's go for a walk along the path, shall we? See if we can spot any holly or twigs for the snowman's arms?"

She winks at me, then pushes Immi's chair through the snow along the canal.

"Time you got a new wheelchair," Te Ariki says.

"Yes," I say, feeling slightly surreal. "Maybe in the New Year I'll talk to the Association."

"No need." He gestures at the doorway leading to the apartment building. A brand-new wheelchair sits out the front, tied with a big red bow. Carl is standing next to it, and he waves as he realizes I've seen him.

"Is he making sure it doesn't get nicked?" I say, acting nonchalant, even though my heart's racing.

Te Ariki chuckles. "Well, I have to admit he carried it down from the car."

"Why have a dog and bark yourself, right?"

His lips twist. "Quite."

I swallow hard. The snow is falling heavily now, coating his shoulders and hair, and landing on my eyelashes as I look up at him. "That sounded flippant, I'm sorry. It's a very generous gift, thank you."

"It's the least I could do." He looks away for a moment, showing me the profile of his unburned side. He's so handsome, with his light-brown skin, black lashes, and black, slightly curly hair. What's he doing here? Has he just come to deliver the chair? Or is he here for some other reason?

He looks back at me, and the warmth in his chocolate-colored eyes could melt the snow. "I want to apologize," he says. He moves closer to me and takes my hands. "Astrid, I'm so terribly sorry. First, for insulting you by offering you money for sex. I did it because I wanted you, and I didn't think you'd sleep with me unless I made it impossible for you not to. I knew it was wrong, though, and I did it anyway, and I'm ashamed of myself."

I rub my nose, which is icy cold. "It's okay."

"And secondly," he continues as if I haven't spoken, "I'm sorry for assuming you'd react to my scars the same way that my ex did. That was unfair of me."

"It's okay," I say again.

"It's not." His brows draw together. "Last night... I had a great time, and I ruined it by overreacting."

"You did, a bit," I admit. "You're quite the drama queen."

He gives me a pained look. "I spoiled the evening, and I'm incredibly sorry for that."

"You asked me not to look, and I broke my promise. I understand."

"Don't forgive me, Astrid," he whispers. "I can't bear it. You have such a huge heart, and I'm such a small man."

"You've just given ten million pounds to charity," I say with a laugh. "How on earth can that make you think you're a small man?"

"It's just money. Linc… he said I'm like a medieval Catholic trying to buy his way out of purgatory. That I'm trying to buy redemption."

"Are you?"

"Maybe."

"Because Hemi died, and you feel responsible?"

"Yes, partly. Maybe because I feel guilty for all the wealth I have. I was born into it, Astrid. I've never known hardship. I can easily spend thousands of pounds on Champagne and whisky and cologne and food. And then you come into my club, willing to work in the kitchen even though you'd already worked all day. And you were so grateful for the opportunity to dance because it paid more money."

"That's not the only reason," I tell him. "I got to spend time with you."

He frowns. "Really?"

"Of course. It doesn't matter how much money a man offered me to go to bed with him. If I didn't like him, I couldn't do it. I only said yes because it was you."

"But you gave it all back."

I shrug. "It didn't seem right to take it when I'd broken my promise."

He swallows and blows out a breath that mists in front of his face. "Linc said I should grovel. Would you like me to get on my knees? Because I will."

I smile. "It's far too cold for that. You don't need to grovel. You just have to mean it when you say sorry."

"I am sorry. From the bottom of my heart."

"I know."

He moves closer to me and brushes a snowflake away when it falls on my cheek. "I like your hair up," he murmurs.

"It's just a scruffy bun."

"You still look like an angel."

"But I'm made for sin, right?"

He strokes his thumb across my bottom lip. "I'm so sorry."

I lift up onto my tiptoes, hold his lapels, and press my lips to his.

We kiss slowly, the snow continuing to fall on our hair and coats, and his lips are warm, although our faces are cold. I open my mouth to his tongue, and my body stirs at the memory of where kisses like this can lead—to Champagne, and warm fires, and lovemaking that sets me alight.

When he eventually moves back, he says, "Will you go out with me?"

My eyebrows lift. "What?"

"On a date. A proper one. I'd like to take you to dinner tonight. I want to get to know you properly."

I know he's hardly gone out since his accident, so I understand how much courage it's taken him to say that. "You're not doing anything else?"

"No. Linc was going to come over and help me finish off the bottle of whisky I started last night. But he won't mind if I see you instead."

But then I remember what's happening this evening. "I can't, I'm afraid," I reply, biting my lip. "We're all going over to my best friend, Cora's, for dinner, and then we're going to watch *It's a Wonderful Life*."

He chuckles. "I haven't seen that in years."

I hesitate. Then I say, "Would you like to come? Cora would love to meet you…" My voice trails off as embarrassment floods me. The guy's a billionaire. The last thing he's going to want to do is be with people he doesn't know.

But to my surprise, he says, "I'd love to."

"Really?"

"Don't look so surprised. I don't have any family in the UK. It'll be nice to share yours. Are you sure Cora won't mind?"

I smile and shake my hand. "I know she won't."

"What time?"

"Six p.m. It's early for a party, but it's so Immi can have some fun. Then she'll crash out on Cora's bed for a couple of hours and we can all get drunk."

He grins. "Six p.m. it is."

"I'll text you the address." Something occurs to me then. "What about Linc? What will he do without you?"

"He's a big boy. He'll manage. He'll probably work, knowing him."

"Aw. Nobody should be alone at Christmas. I'm going to call him and ask him if he'd like to come, too."

He chuckles. "If you want." He glances around as Mum approaches, pushing Immi's wheelchair.

"I'm sorry," she apologizes, "but Immi's getting cold."

"Te Ariki has bought you a new wheelchair," I say, gesturing to where it sits by the apartment door.

Mum's eyes widen, and Immi's jaw drops. "Thank you," Immi says. Her face is a picture as Te Ariki beckons the security guard, and he wheels it toward us. "Oh, it's pink!" she says. "I love it!"

Te Ariki chuckles. "Would you like to sit in it?"

"Please." She lifts her arms, and my breath catches in my throat as he bends, picks her up easily, and carries her over to the new chair. "Even the wheels are pink," she says in wonder, "and there's tinsel around the arms!"

"That was me," Te Ariki said. "It seemed right at Christmas." He places her in it, making sure she's comfortable, then smiles at us. "I'll carry the chair up to your flat for you, and Carl will carry the old one, unless you want me to take it away for you?"

"That would be great, thank you—I don't have anywhere to put it."

So Carl takes the old chair to his car, and Te Ariki brings up the new one while I carry Immi.

"We need to get that elevator fixed," he says firmly. "I'll call the council."

"You needn't…" I stop speaking as he gives me a look. "Okay."

Once we're inside, Te Ariki promises to return at six to pick us all up, and with a brief final kiss on my lips, he leaves.

I close the door behind him and turn to face Mum and Immi. They're both watching with big smiles, and I press my fingers to my lips.

"Aw," Mum says as I run over to them and fling my arms around both of them. "It's all right, sweetheart," she says. "It's about time Santa gave you something nice for Christmas."

Epilogue

Linc

The Uber pulls up at the house on Primrose Hill, and I get out into the cold December air.

Regent's Park is just across the road, and it looks like a winter wonderland, the grass and trees thick with snow that sparkles in the moonlight. It's stopped snowing for a while, and the clouds have parted to reveal an almost-full moon, hanging in the sky like a Christmas bauble.

I lift the hamper out of the back of the car, then thank the driver and cross to number sixty-two. I'm a little late, and Te Ariki's Aston Martin is sitting out the front, which is a relief. It's never fun going to a party where you don't know anyone, and I was tempted to turn Astrid down when she called me.

But the truth is that I don't have anything else planned tonight. I could have gone down into the club, where I'm sure I would have spotted friends or business acquaintances. And I could have called several other married friends and asked if they'd mind if I dropped in for the evening. But most of them are busy with their partners and families.

When I was fourteen, after my father put me in hospital by hitting me with a golf club, the authorities got me a place at Greenfield—a school for troubled youths run by Atticus Bell in the South Island of New Zealand. During the school holidays, most kids went home to their families. The first year I was there, I was put with a foster family, but once I became friends with Atticus's children, and I started spending most of my free time at the family's house on the grounds, Atticus's wife, Clemmie, suggested I stay with them for Christmas, and I was quick to agree.

SERENITY WOODS

As I go through the gate and walk up the path to the front door, my mind flashes back to my last Christmas there. It was the height of summer Down Under, of course—I still can't get used to it being cold in December—and Clemmie and Atticus cooked Christmas dinner on the barbecue, and we ate it sitting out on the deck. Here in the UK the sun sets before 4 p.m. at this time of year, but in New Zealand it doesn't set until 9 p.m., and everyone stays outdoors, eating, drinking, talking, and playing games until late.

Atticus was a deacon and the school chaplain, and his family went to a late service at the local church. I'm not religious at all, but I used to go with them because I liked the carols and the story of the Nativity, and the feeling of community. Now, when I hear a choir sing *O Little Town of Bethlehem* or *Once in Royal David's City*, I'm transported back to that last evening, of sitting next to Elora-Rose Bell in the pew, and holding her hand down by our sides so nobody could see.

I loved her. I know that now. For the first few years after I left New Zealand, I told myself it was just a childhood crush, but that does a disservice to the feelings I had for her. Still have, if I'm honest. Not that they do me any good. I have no plans to return to New Zealand, and wouldn't be able to see her even if I did. No, the ghost of Christmas past can show me memories of her bright-blonde hair and mischievous eyes as much as it likes. I won't be going back.

I knock on the door, and it opens almost immediately to reveal a pretty brunette wearing a red T-shirt with an owl in a Christmas hat and the words "I'm on the naughty list and I regret nothing."

"You must be Linc!" she says, beaming a smile at me.

"Cora?"

"Yes, come in! I'm so glad you could make it."

I squeeze past her with the hamper, and she closes the door behind me. "I hope you don't mind me gatecrashing," I say.

"Of course not, the more the merrier."

"I brought some supplies."

"Ooh, that wasn't necessary but thank you! Go straight down to the kitchen, and you can put them in there."

I go into the kitchen and put the hamper on one of the chairs around the central pine table with a groan, as it's very heavy. Cora peers in it and says, "Wow! Oh my God, Linc, you can come again."

I chuckle. It contains a pile of Christmas goodies from Fortnum & Mason—a few bottles of wine, a variety of special biscuits or cookies, champagne truffles, festive nuts, liqueur chocolates, and a host of other festive treats.

"Darren," she says as a rather ordinary-looking guy comes into the kitchen, "look at what Linc's brought."

"Hello," he says, shaking my hand, and then his eyes widen as he peers into the box. "Ooh. Peppermint bark."

I grin. "Help yourself. The reindeer noses are for Immi, though."

He takes them out and gives them to me. "She's in the living room with the others."

"Okay, thanks." I go through the other doorway into the dining room, past the table that's groaning with food, and into the living room.

A sofa and chairs face a roaring log fire, and a Christmas tree stands in the corner, a real tree, reaching to the ceiling and twinkling with fairy lights.

Te Ariki is standing to one side, talking to a guy wearing an ugly festive sweater, and he raises a hand as he sees me. "Linc!"

I cross over to them, and Te Ariki and I exchange a bearhug. I'm glad to see that although he's wearing his mask, he hasn't got his hoodie on with the hood pulled up. I think Astrid is going to be good for him.

I smile at the guy in the sweater, who says, "I'm Alan, I'm Cora's brother-in-law."

"Pleased to meet you." I shake hands with him, then with his wife, Ruth, and with Astrid's mother. I say hello to Immi and give her the reindeer noses.

Then I smile at Astrid, who rises and gives me a hug. "I'm so glad you came," she says.

"Thank you for asking me." I glance at Te Ariki and murmur, "How's he doing?"

"He seems okay. He's getting through the day, anyway, and tomorrow it'll be done, and it'll start getting easier."

"I think his life will be a lot easier now," I reply, "but it's nothing to do with the time of year." I smile at her. She's wearing a headband with an angel's halo. "It's a bit bent," I point out.

"Te Ariki likes it like that," she says mischievously, and I laugh.

"Grub's up!" Cora announces. "Come and help yourself."

She and Darren have put on a buffet-style meal with filled rolls and sandwiches, tiny pies and sausage rolls, chips and crudites and lots of dips, mince pies and Christmas cake, and a big jug of hot mulled wine.

We all pile up our plates, then find a seat in the living room, and she puts on *It's a Wonderful Life*.

I sit on a beanbag and eat while I watch the old movie, glancing from time to time at Te Ariki and Astrid, who are sitting side by side on the sofa. He has his arm around her, and she's positively glowing, teasing him and making him laugh, which warms my heart. The guy has been to hell and back, and he deserves a happy ever after. I think about when I saw his plane go down, and how I felt when I saw that his brother was dead and I pulled Te Ariki out of the flames. I was there, too, when Sara May walked into his hospital room and recoiled in horror. I knew that would scar him worse than the fire, and could never have envisaged that he might find love just a year later.

My phone buzzes in my jeans pocket, announcing a call. I pull it out, assuming it's one of my friends, then stare at the screen as I see the name, Sean. It's my brother in New Zealand. I haven't spoken to him since I left the country, ten years ago. We keep in touch occasionally by email, and we exchanged mobile numbers a couple of years ago, but he's never called me before.

I rise, go out into the kitchen, and answer the call. "Hello?"

"Linc? It's Sean."

"Hey. Merry Christmas." I speak a little stiffly. Sean continued to live with our parents after I left and went to Greenfield. I don't know why he was never the target of Dad's violence and vitriol. Although I know Dad's attitude to me wasn't Sean's fault, it would have been inhuman of me if I hadn't felt some resentment toward him for being Dad's favorite.

"Yes, of course. I forgot it was Christmas," he says.

My eyebrows rise. "What do you mean? I assumed that was why you were calling."

"No… Linc, I'm calling to let you know that Dad's very sick."

My gaze drifts out of the window. The clouds have covered the moon, and it's started to snow again. "What's wrong with him?"

"He has lung cancer. He only found out in August. It's progressed really quickly. They think he only has a few weeks to live. And I thought I should let you know, just in case… well… I thought you might want to come and see him before… you know…" His voice fades away.

I don't remember Don Green ever giving me a hug or a kind word. Every single memory I have of him is filled with cruelty and violence, or at best, complete disinterest. I haven't heard a word from him since I left.

I think about how he once held my arm over a hot stove and burned it. How he frequently gave me backhanders across the face, and hit me on the back with his belt. It was because of him that I turned into a moody, rebellious, badly behaved teenager who smoked and stole and got into trouble with the police. And I can still remember the relief I felt after he hit me with the golf club, before I fell unconscious, because I knew he'd gone too far, and that it meant I'd finally be free of him.

"Fuck him," I say to Sean. "Let me know when he's dead, and I'll come back and dance on his grave." I end the call, and stuff the phone back into my pocket.

I lean on the kitchen sink, looking out at the garden, my hands curling into fists. I want to yell or smash something, to vent the anger that is bottled up inside me. I feel furious indignation because I'm upset, and I don't want to be upset that my fucking father is dying. He doesn't deserve my grief, and I refuse to let it out.

Gradually, the intensity of my feelings dies away, and my finger unfurl.

I turn and walk back to the living room doorway, and lean on the wall for a moment. Te Ariki is murmuring something to Astrid, and I watch as he kisses behind her ear, and she shivers. I feel a pang of envy, even though I'm pleased for him. Even though I've had a few girlfriends, I've yet to meet my Astrid, and I know part of the reason is because I gave my heart to another girl years ago.

My words to Sean about going back were said sarcastically, but I realize that I could go back for my father's funeral. And while I was in New Zealand, I could catch up with Joel and Fraser, Atticus's sons.

And I could see Elora-Rose.

My heart bangs at the thought. She was fourteen the last time I saw her. I've deliberately not looked her up on social media over the years. I knew it would be too hard to see her growing up, in photos with other guys, maybe getting married, having children. I've tried to move on.

Hell, what's the point in going to see her? Even if she's not married… even if she's single… it would only be a fleeting visit, and it's not as if it could lead to anything.

But I realize that even if she's with someone else, I still want to see her again. I want to see Fraser and Joel. And I want to see the country I was born in. I've traveled a lot, and I've had a great time working on excavations across the world, but I haven't been able to put down any roots because deep down, my heart remains in New Zealand.

Te Ariki glances over his shoulder, sees me, and says, "Everything okay?"

I smile and nod, go back into the room, and sit on the beanbag. In the movie, James Stewart is close to discovering the true meaning of Christmas, and Immi is watching with wide eyes as he makes his way back to the bridge, where the angel, Clarence, is about to do his magic and return him to the proper timeline.

Astrid slides her arm around Te Ariki's waist, and he kisses the top of her head beneath her halo. It looks as if their Christmas wishes have come true.

Silently, I make one of my own, as the bell rings, and Clarence gets his wings.

Seduction Under the Southern Stars

If you loved *One Night before Christmas* and you're interested in discovering what happens to Linc when he goes back to New Zealand for his father's funeral, you can read his story in the first of the Southern Stars series, *Seduction Under the Southern Stars*.

*

She's strictly off-limits, but that only makes me want her more.

When my old friend, Joel, asks me to stay in New Zealand and help his little sister search for a long-lost family heirloom, I'm tempted to say no. Returning home for my father's funeral has stirred up memories I'd rather forget, and I'm eager to escape back to my luxurious life in Europe.

But only I know the location of the treasure she's hunting, and I owe her family a debt I can't ignore. Nine years ago, I was the troubled boy who made the mistake of kissing the deacon's daughter—an innocent kiss that got me banished by her furious father. I never forgot that kiss. Turns out, neither did she.

Elora's all grown up now: stunning, smart, and a hell of a lot tougher. Joel made sure I know she's still out of bounds, but I've never been good at following rules.

Ten days alone with her under the southern stars. Ten days to break down her defenses, to seduce her into reliving that forbidden kiss—and maybe more. Well, resisting temptation has never been my style...

*

Sample - Chapter One

Friday, January 26th

Elora

"Love Under the Southern Stars." My older brother, Fraser, swipes his hand from left to right in front of him to illustrate how the title would form a banner. "What do you think?"

Zoe, sitting next to me, blows a raspberry. "Boring! Let's do an exhibition called Murder Under the Southern Stars. That would be much more interesting."

"But less suitable for Valentine's Day," Fraser points out.

"Not where my exes are concerned," Zoe mumbles, and I giggle.

"It sounds great," I tell him. "I'm sure it'll be really popular."

The National Museum of New Zealand in Wellington isn't the country's biggest museum, but since Fraser became director, it's grown in both size and prestige due mainly to his vision and hard work. I joined him after graduating from university and have worked here for a couple of years now. I adore the historic building that sits right on the Wellington waterfront, with its elegant entrance framed by marble pillars and its curved staircase, and I especially love the conservation room, where we X-ray, clean, and treat archaeological artifacts. If I had more bookshelves and an endless supply of coffee and Jaffa Cakes, I could live here.

"Hallie," Fraser says as another young woman enters the room, "come and join us. I was just telling the others about my idea for a new exhibition."

"Oh, cool." She draws up a stool at the table and sits beside me.

Hallie, Zoe, and I are part of the museum archaeology team. The three of us couldn't be more different in both looks and personality, but we've formed a firm friendship, and work together well. Hallie is in her late twenties, sophisticated and calm, with long brown hair and gentle brown eyes. Zoe is the same age as me, twenty-four, with black hair cut in a quirky bob and flashing green eyes, and she's outspoken and feisty, but she has a heart of gold.

I'm blonde, blue-eyed, and quiet, and can usually be found with my nose stuck in a book. That's about it, really.

"Love Under the Southern Stars," Fraser repeats for Hallie's benefit.

"Do the thing," Zoe tells him. "With the banner."

He says the words more dramatically, this time sweeping his hand across in front of him with a theatrical gesture.

"Sounds amazing," Hallie says.

"I thought the centerpiece could be the Hatfield Love Letter," he announces, naming a document the museum acquired recently, written by a captain who won the Victoria Cross in the New Zealand wars of the nineteenth century. "And then I'd like each of you to find me a new artifact for the exhibition."

"What?" I stare at him.

"Yes, Elora, which means actually leaving the museum and going out to talk to real, live people."

"I'd rather not."

"Even so. I'm sure the three of you will come up with some amazing pieces if you put your minds to it. You haven't got long, so you'd better get a move on."

"And they've got to be romance-related," Hallie confirms.

"For this exhibition, yes. Either newly excavated artifacts, or you can apply to get something on loan from another museum."

"So you mean, like, Rasputin's knob or something," Zoe suggests, opening a pack of Maltesers.

He gives her a patient look. "Zoe…"

"It's floating in a pickle jar somewhere in St. Petersburg," she insists, offering him the pack.

He takes one. "As much as I'd be interested in seeing the preserved appendage of Russia's greatest love machine, I was hoping for something a little more… romantic."

"I'm sure Queen Victoria's vibrator is in the British Museum," Hallie teases, also taking one. "I think it's steam powered."

He rolls his eyes as we all start laughing. "I should've known better than to bring up a topic like this."

"Maybe we'll just put you in the exhibit," I suggest, accepting a Malteser and popping it in my mouth.

Fraser looks down at himself. He's wearing brown corduroy trousers and a tweed jacket with leather patches on the elbows. A pair of round spectacles sits on his nose. He's only just turned thirty, and he's gorgeous, but he does insist on dressing as if he's time-traveled from Victorian England.

He looks back at us. Hallie presses her lips together, trying not to laugh. Zoe grins openly.

"What are you implying?" he asks indignantly.

"Nothing at all," Hallie soothes. "Anyway, I think I might apply to borrow the Venus de Willendorf from Vienna. Although I'll probably get asked if I modeled for it."

That makes us all chuckle. The Venus figurine, which is nearly thirty thousand years old, portrays a woman with... how do I say it politely... big boobs and wide hips. Hallie is curvy, but she doesn't have quite the same proportions as the figurine.

"Not at all," Fraser says, "You're not... I mean you have very..." Her eyes gleam, and he gives up and clears his throat. "Well, you only have two weeks before Valentine's Day," he continues, "so get your thinking caps on. I was planning to..." His voice trails off as he looks behind us, and his eyes widen. We all turn to follow his gaze.

For the first time in my life, I do a double take, and I inhale sharply.

A man stands in the doorway. He's wearing a black suit with a white shirt and a black tie, and he looks like James Bond, a stark contrast to Fraser in his tweed and the three of us girls in our casual clothing. He's tall, the same height as Fraser, so probably six-two, broad shouldered, and drop-dead handsome. Something about him suggests he's wealthy—the cut of his suit, maybe, his fancy tie pin, or the way his dark hair is styled with a fashionable fade. He's clean shaven, his jaw so smooth it wouldn't surprise me if he'd used a cut-throat razor. He also has the greenest eyes I think I've ever seen, a light sage color, so striking I can see them from across the room.

I haven't seen him for ten years, but it's unmistakably the guy who broke my heart when I was a girl.

He's staring at me, but he doesn't look shocked, just... interested. He knew I was here.

My head spins, and I feel faint as all the blood rushes from my brain. I don't want to think about where it's going.

"Linc!" Fraser strides across the room and throws his arms around the guy.

Linc holds his arms out to the side for a moment as if surprised at Fraser's reaction, then laughs and wraps them around him, and the two men exchange a bearhug.

"Bro," Fraser says, releasing him, "I didn't know you'd arrived."

Wait, what? Fraser knew he was coming?

"Got in yesterday," Linc replies. His voice was deep back then, but it's huskier now, more mature. He's grown from a boy into a man.

I've thought of him so much over the years, wondering what happened to him, and what he looks like today. I know my other brother kept in touch with him, but after what happened I didn't want to ask any questions, and I certainly couldn't ask my father. So just like the One Ring, history became legend, and legend became myth, and while Linc didn't exactly pass out of all knowledge, he's preserved in my mind as if in amber, forever eighteen, so it's a huge shock to see him grown up.

I knew he would have filled out. Developed real facial hair rather than the bum fluff he sported back then. Probably lost the intense earnestness of youth, become more serious, more cynical. But would he have become less passionate about the things that mattered to us in those days? Or lost the spirit of adventure I'd found so attractive in him?

Did he think of me at all? I had no way of knowing.

Judging by the look on his face as Fraser steps back and Linc looks at me, he hasn't forgotten me. He opens his mouth to say something, but turns as, behind him, my other brother, Joel, appears at a run, skidding to a stop as he sees the scene.

"Ah," Joel says, "I wondered where you'd gone." He looks at me and frowns. Joel is twenty-eight and an underwater archaeologist, which goes some way to explaining why his hair always looks as if he's just dried it with a towel.

So Joel knew Linc was here too. My brothers were obviously hoping to ensure we didn't meet.

Does my father know he's here?

"I was looking for Fraser," Linc says. "I didn't realize… there would be other people here." He looks at me. I know it's a lie.

I can feel Zoe and Hallie looking at me curiously, but I keep my gaze fixed on him as Fraser walks toward us and Linc follows.

"Let me introduce you," Fraser says smoothly. "This is Hallie Woodford, and this is Zoe Moon, two of the museum's archaeologists. Ladies, this is Lincoln Green."

"And before you ask, no, I wasn't named after the color of Robin Hood's tights," Linc says, holding out his hand to Zoe.

Her lips curve up as she slides her hand into his. Two seconds in, and he's already charmed her. He hasn't changed a bit.

"Hello…" she says with interest, about an inch from tweaking her bow tie and saying, 'Ding, dong!' like an actor from the 1950s.

"Hello, Zoe, pleased to meet you." He turns to Hallie. "And hi, Hallie."

"Linc," she says warmly, "I'm so excited to meet you. I've never met a real divvy!"

My eyebrows rise. "A what?"

"A divvy," she replies. "You know. A diviner? It's usually used in antiques. It means someone with the ability to find artifacts or distinguish fakes or forgeries from the genuine article."

My jaw drops. "What?"

She laughs as Linc's lips twist. "He works for iDigBritain. They made a program about him last year, singing his praises. Jeez, Elora, you didn't see it? He's quite famous."

I'm not surprised. There was always something exceptional about him. I am shocked that he's here, though. Standing in front of me looking so… real.

He walks up to me. "Hello, Lora," he says softly. He always used to call me that, or occasionally add my middle name, Elora-Rose.

"Hello, Linc." Should I shake his hand? I look into his eyes, and then he smiles, and I can't help it—I lift my arms around his neck, and he wraps his arms around my waist. He squeezes, tight enough to force the air out of me, and lifts my feet off the ground a fraction before lowering me back down.

"It's good to see you," he whispers, releasing me.

Touching him scrambles my brain, like an egg whisked with a fork on a hot plate, and I step back, head spinning. "So… um… you did become an archaeologist?" I say breathlessly, conscious of the others watching.

"I did," he says. "Thanks to you." He glances at my brothers. "And your family."

"He discovered the Framlingham Hoard," Hallie says. "It was the second largest hoard of Roman coins ever found in the UK. Over ten thousand coins, wasn't it?"

"Yeah," Linc says, "nearly fourteen thousand."

"You must have made a fortune from that find," Zoe says, mouth open.

"Zoe," Hallie scolds.

"That's all right, I don't mind," he says. "The British Museum bought them for 1.75 million pounds, split between me and the landowner."

"And you found the Heacham Hoard too, didn't you?" Hallie continues. "All those Iron Age torcs and bracelets. The article said you had a nose for gold."

"The Midas Touch," he says, and smiles.

Oh my God, I didn't know any of this. I read a lot of books, but I'm not as well-versed in today's archaeology news as Hallie.

There's an awkward silence as the others watch Linc and me stare at each other. There's so much I want to say, so many questions I want to ask, and yet my lips refuse to form a single word.

Eventually, maybe sensing how flustered I feel, Zoe rests a comforting hand in the middle of my back as she says to him, "I'd ask if you want to help clean some artifacts, but you look as if you're going to a funeral."

"I am, as it happens," he says. "In an hour, so I should get going soon."

"Shit." Zoe looks aghast. "I'm so sorry. I'm always putting my foot in it."

"Not at all."

"Is that why you're in New Zealand?" I ask him, wondering whose death would bring him back.

Linc nods. "I wanted to make sure they nailed the coffin shut." It's a throwaway comment, said with some amusement, but bitterness drips from the words.

"Your father died?" I conclude.

He nods again, sliding his hands into the pockets of his trousers.

I stare at him, tongue-tied. I feel that I should say I'm sorry, except I'm not, and he obviously isn't, either. But even though at times I'm sure we've both wished his dad was obliterated from existence, nobody remains unscarred by the death of their father, and he must be dealing with a confusing array of emotions right now.

Fraser clears his throat. "We were just discussing our next exhibition."

"Love Under the Southern Stars," Hallie says, swiping her hand in front of her the same way Fraser did. "For Valentine's Day."

"I'm going to ask to borrow Rasputin's knob," Zoe announces, "and Hallie's going to source Queen Victoria's steam-powered vibrator."

Joel snorts. Linc laughs. The gap in his front two teeth where one of them was a little twisted has disappeared, and now they're beautifully straight. His eyes sparkle when they meet mine. "So what artifact are you going to bring?"

"Fraser's only just told us about it," I reply, "so I haven't had much chance to think yet."

"Shame you never found the Bell Ring." Joel steals the last Malteser from Zoe's packet, prompting her to glare at him.

At Hallie's curious look, I say, "Our great-great…"

"Two more greats," Joel says.

"Three more," Fraser corrects.

"Okay," I continue, "four or five greats-grandfather—called Atticus, same as my dad—fell in love with a Māori girl during the Gold Rush of the 1860s. The story goes that she told him she'd only marry him if he gave her a ring containing a piece of greenstone from her birthplace in Milford Sound." Greenstone is also known as jade or, in Māori, *pounamu*. "He sailed from Christchurch around to Fiordland and took one of the perilous mountain trails, where he personally fished a piece of greenstone out from the river there and he had it set in a ring made from the gold he mined near Arrowtown. Legend says as soon as she laid eyes on the ring, she fell in love with him, because he'd gone to so much trouble to make it. After that the ring was supposed to grant true love to whoever touched it."

"It went missing though," Fraser says, "sometime in the mid-twentieth century."

I look at Linc, wondering if he remembers the story. I told him about it one rainy afternoon in the living room of our house at Greenfield. I was ten at the time, and he was fourteen, and he'd only recently started at the school. I'd constructed a tent from one of my mother's sheets, and I was lying beneath it, reading a book about the history of my family, when Linc ducked under the flap of the tent, flopped to the ground beside me, and said, "Whatcha reading?"

He'd known practically nothing about history at the time, and, used to spending his time smoking, drinking, or stealing from shops, he'd laughed at my dusty books and atlases. But that day I must have spoken with passion about my family history, because he'd pulled the book toward him and started flicking through the pages. "Where's Milford Sound?" he'd asked when he read the story. I'd dragged out an old atlas, and we'd scoured the mountains and valleys of the South Island together.

"I remember," he says now, obviously following my train of thought. "That's where it all began. I have you to thank for that."

Our eyes lock, and a shock passes through me like static, so sharp and fast I'm surprised my hair doesn't stand out from my head. For a moment, it's as if no time has passed at all, and nothing has changed. He's still the handsome boy with the startling green eyes that I fell in love with, and I'm still the young girl he kissed.

Then Joel coughs, breaking the spell, and I blink and drop my gaze. What am I thinking? Everything's changed. My heart was like a priceless Greek urn, and Linc dropped it and fractured it into a hundred pieces and left them lying on the ground. He left, and I never heard a single word from him. I had to pick up the pieces myself, one at a time, and glue them back into some semblance of the shape it once was. But it hasn't been the same since. Other men have only weakened those cracks, so you can still see the lines where it broke. It remains so fragile that I keep it locked up like the priceless artifact it was. A once-beautiful treasure, now sitting on a plinth in a glass cage with a light shining on it, meant to be viewed, not handled. Never to be touched again.

"I might know where the Bell Ring is," Linc says.

My gaze snaps back up to his. "What?" Joel and Fraser also stare at him.

"A couple of years ago, I was at a conference in Rome," Linc says, "and I met an Australian archaeologist called Graham Tucker. We were talking about family heirlooms, and I mentioned the Bell Ring. It turned out that he had a colleague who said a friend of his acquired what he thought was the Bell Ring in the 1990s. He ran an antique shop."

I blink as I try to sift through the complicated trail of relationships. "Oh my God, Linc! Can you remember the name of the guy or his friend?"

"No, sorry." He checks his watch again. "Look, I really have to go, but if you like I can come back afterward, and we can talk about it some more."

Joel and Fraser exchange a glance. They know how I fell apart after Linc left, and I'm sure they're worried about what effect his being here will have on me. That's why they didn't tell me he was coming. But it's been ten years. I've moved on. I'm not the innocent girl I was. I'm not going to fall at his feet at the snap of his fingers again. I've learned my lesson.

And anyway, it would be amazing if he was able to track down the Bell Ring. Oh my God, imagine Mum's face—it would mean so much to her.

"If that's okay," I say to Linc, "it would be great to catch up."

He nods. "All right, I'll probably be an hour or so, I'd imagine."

"You're not going back to the house afterward?" Joel asks.

Linc gives him an amused look. "I might not even make it into the church. I just want to check the old fucker's really dead."

That's a touch of the old Linc rising to the surface, and it makes me smile.

"See ya," he says, and, with a last glance at me, he walks away, out of the room.

Joel hesitates, then follows him out.

Hallie turns to me, eyes wide. "Oh my God, Elora! Why didn't you tell us you knew him?"

I blink, my head spinning. "It was such a long time ago. And I didn't know he was famous. I haven't heard about him or seen him since I was fourteen."

"He's got a Wikipedia page! Have you never Googled him?"

I shake my head. "I've tried not to think about him…" I glance at Fraser, who's frowning, pity in his eyes.

"What happened?" Zoe asks, leaning on the table with wide eyes.

I feel suddenly embarrassed. It felt like the love story of a lifetime back then, but now it feels like a childish crush.

"He was a student at our father's school," Fraser tells them when I don't say anything.

"At Greenfield?" Zoe asks.

I nod. My father runs Greenfield Residential School near Hanmer Springs in the South Island. It's a school for troubled adolescents. Dad—who's a deacon, and the chaplain at Greenfield—holds what he calls adventure therapy programs, which involve taking youths out into the mountains and forests and using team-building techniques to encourage them to talk and work with one another. He's helped so many young people, and I'm immensely proud of him.

He and Mum live in a house on the grounds of the school, and it's where Fraser, Joel, and I grew up. We were encouraged to mix with the students as a kind of civilizing influence, I guess; Dad always hoped our manners and wholesome attitude would brush off on the other kids. Most of the time, he discouraged them from coming to the house, but Linc was a special case.

"What was he like back then?" Hallie asks.

"He was fourteen when he came to the school. I was ten." I think back to the first time I met him. He was already tall, with flashing green eyes and a rebellious glare. "He was gorgeous even then," I admit. His face had borne scars from where his father had beaten him so badly that he'd put him in hospital, but I don't tell the girls that.

"How long was he at Greenfield?" Zoe wants to know.

"Four years," Fraser says. "He wasn't interested in archaeology when he first arrived, but he spent a lot of time at the house with us, so he was bound to get hooked."

Archaeology is my father's second love after the church, and he instilled a passion for it in all his children, as well as many of the kids who came to the school.

Zoe looks from Fraser to me and back again. "So... what happened?" She can obviously sense there's more to the story.

Fraser slides his hands into his pockets and doesn't say anything.

"We spent a lot of time together," I say, somewhat flatly. "I had a crush on him, and... well, I'm not sure what his feelings were for me. One afternoon, he kissed me. But we didn't realize my father was watching."

Zoe's jaw drops. "Oh shit."

"He went ballistic." I shudder at the memory. My father doesn't get angry very often, which is probably why I found his white-hot rage so upsetting at the time.

"You were only fourteen," Fraser reminds me, "and Linc was eighteen."

"I wasn't pre-pubescent," I say sarcastically. "If this was medieval England I would have been married with six kids by then."

"Dad saw Linc as another son and thought he was abusing that relationship," Fraser says.

"We weren't related," I reply hotly, pissed off that he's defending Dad, and that he didn't tell me Linc was coming here.

"That's not what I mean," he replies with irritating calmness. "Dad invested a lot of time and affection in him, and he trusted him. He thought Linc was taking advantage of you."

"It was one kiss!"

"But that might have led to more, and you were Dad's baby girl."

"There's no 'were' about it," I grumble, because our father still treats me as if I'm a kid.

"What happened?" Hallie asks.

"It was late-ish in the day, and Dad sent me to my room, so I went to bed." I cried myself to sleep, although I don't tell them that. "When I got up the next morning, Linc had gone. Apparently, he contacted TAG18 and asked them to send him wherever they had a vacancy." The Archaeology Group finds places for students on excavations all across the world. "I think they sent him to Egypt. That's all I know. I never heard from him again."

"Oh, Elora…" Hallie's voice is soft. "I'm so sorry."

"No wonder you were shocked to see him," Zoe says.

I force a laugh as Fraser lifts a brow. "Oh, it was a long time ago now. It was hard, but I got over him. I assumed he'd stayed in Europe somewhere. I didn't even think to look him up."

The truth is, though, that I didn't want to know. I didn't want to see him on Facebook or Instagram, and look at photos of him living another, better life. Of him with other women. I didn't think I could bear it. He'd gone, and I had a feeling he wouldn't be coming back. Why would he, for a fourteen-year-old girl with whom he'd exchanged one single kiss? I was young, but I thought enough of myself to be determined not to pine for him forever.

So I pushed him to the back of my mind, where he has remained like an old book on a shelf, gathering dust.

But I've never gotten over him. And now he's back, looking a thousand times more handsome.

Oh my. How am I going to cope?

Seduction Under the Southern Stars is the first in the Southern Stars series.

Newsletter

If you'd like to be informed when my next book is available,
you can sign up for my mailing list on my website,
http://www.serenitywoodsromance.com

About the Author

USA Today bestselling author Serenity Woods writes sexy contemporary romances, most of which are set in the sub-tropical Northland of New Zealand, where she lives with her wonderful husband.

Website: http://www.serenitywoodsromance.com
Facebook: http://www.facebook.com/serenitywoodsromance

Printed in Great Britain
by Amazon

56907788R00071